AMELIA FANG
and the
TROUBLE WITH TOADS

LAURA ELLEN ANDERSON

EGMONT

CONTENTS

Ghoulish Greetings!

AMELIA FANG

LIKES:
Birthnight parties
Making eyecrust models

DISLIKES:
When her brother eats her clothes
When her brother breaks her things

VINCENT

LIKES:
Eating mashed brain
Throwing mashed brain

DISLIKES:
Being clean and tidy
Being quiet

GRIMALDI

LIKES:
Learning about toads
Listening to his frien

DISLIKES:
Squished toad alerts
His friends being ups

FLORENCE

LIKES:
Prancing to save the day
Playing zombie tag

DISLIKES:
Being called a BEAST!
Annoying toads

TANGINE

LIKES:
New shoes for adventures
Half price bow ties

DISLIKES:
His friends being in danger
His hair being out of place

FREDA

LIKES:
Baking cakes and rolls
Pink houses

DISLIKES:
Snot or mess
A bad cake

MAJESTIC TOAD

LIKES:
Perfection
Her brother

DISLIKES:
Anything less than perfect
Not seeing her brother

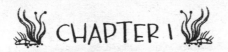

CHAPTER 1

THE FRANKENFLU

It was a particularly misty Friday night in Nocturnia, and young vampire Amelia Fang was getting ready for a fangtastic weekend ahead. Tomorrow was Grimaldi's birthnight! Grimaldi was one of Amelia's best friends in the whole world.

'We're going to enjoy a deadly dinner, then we're going to play games and THEN watch the newest TOADSTAR movie!' Amelia said excitedly to her mother, Countess Frivoleeta. 'And I've made Grimaldi an EXTRA special gift. A model of me, Grimaldi, Florence and

1

Tangine standing under the Petrified-Tree-That-Looks-Like-a-Unicorn.'

'It all sounds delightfully dreadful, my awful little popsicle,' said the countess. She was sitting at the kitchen table feeding Amelia's baby brother Vincent a bowl of mashed brain. It was his favourite dish, mostly because he loved to BOSH the spoon out of his mother's hand and then laugh hysterically. This time he also did a big smelly poo in his nappy.

Amelia was quite looking forward to having a break from her baby brother. Although she loved Vincent VERY MUCH, he was the slimiest, pongiest thing Amelia had ever known. And if the family took their eyes off him for even one second, he would roll away, or climb into the bin or rub his grimy hands over everything.

Yesternight, he'd smeared spider-leg stew over Amelia's limited-edition signed

The Pumpkin Whisperer book. And last week he ate her homework, which was very embarrassing to have to tell her teacher. But at least *this* weekend she wouldn't have to worry about any of that.

Amelia spent the rest of the night packing her pumpkin backpack. But as she took her favourite pumpkin dress off its clothes hanger, she gasped. There was a great big slobbery hole at the bottom! She recognised that slobber: a mixture of mashed brain and snot . . .

'Viiiiiiiinceeeeent!' she cried, stomping down the stairs and into the kitchen. 'Mum! Vincent has chewed a hole in my favourite pumpkin dress! He must have done it when he crawled into the washing machine last week.' She frowned at her little brother, who stretched out his grime-covered arms towards her. 'No hugs for you right now! You've been very naughty!' Amelia slumped on to the kitchen chair. Her pet pumpkin Squashy pa-doinged on to her lap and nuzzled into her belly. 'At least I can rely on *you* not to chew holes in my best clothes,' she muttered.

'Oh, my lovely little boil-burster,' the countess said softly. 'Try not to be cross with your brother. He's only little.'

'But he ruins all my nice stuff!' fumed Amelia. 'I even found bum-prints on my pumpkin magazines!'

The countess stroked Amelia's cheek. 'Your brother might seem very annoying right now, but you'd miss all the snot and sticky patches if he wasn't here.'

'I would NOT,' said Amelia grumpily, as Vincent tipped the entire contents of his lukewarm armpit sweat-shake into his nappy.

'I know he IS a bit messy,' chuckled Countess Frivoleeta. 'But so was another little vampire I know when she was a baby.' She winked. 'Plus, you love to make a mess in your bedroom when you're working on your pumpkin creations.'

'That's *different*,' said Amelia. 'I'm making a mess for a reason. THEN I tidy it up.'

The countess smiled. 'Be patient, darkling. He's not doing it on purpose.' She gave Amelia a kiss on the head. 'He adores you, you know.'

Vincent blinked at Amelia, then ripped off his nappy and threw it across the room.

'Anyway, at least you will have an amazing weekend with your friends,' said the countess. 'I've got a million things to do, what with your father and Wooo stuck in bed with the Frankenflu. They've gone through almost thirty-nine boxes of tissues between them in two days!'

The next moonrise, Amelia was gobbling down her Unlucky Arms cereal, ready to rush off to Grimaldi's birthnight party. She couldn't wait for a whole weekend of brother-free fun!

Countess Frivoleeta hobbled into the kitchen. Her usual beehive hairdo was looking more like a bird's nest and she was wrapped up in a velvet dressing gown. 'Darkling,' she croaked. 'I think I've caught the – the – the – ACHOO!'

'Oh no!' said Amelia. 'You've got the Frankenflu too?'

'I'm afraid so, my little nugget of flesh,'

said the countess, blowing her nose and making her eyeballs bulge. 'Could you be a darkling and look after Vincent?'

Amelia looked at her mother with horror. 'But it's Grimaldi's birthnight!' she cried.

'I'm so sorry, darkling,' said Countess Frivoleeta. 'Could you take Vincent with you? I'm going to have to go to bed. And I'd hate for either of you to catch this yucky Frankenflu.'

Amelia sighed.

It was the last thing she wanted, but she knew she had to help her mum out. 'No worries,' she said quietly. 'It'll be totally fine . . .'

Out of the corner of her eye, Amelia spotted a stream of yellow liquid flying through the air. Just in time, she picked up the nearest saucepan and used it as a wee catcher. '*Totally fine*,' she said with a very strained smile.

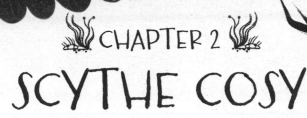

❦ CHAPTER 2 ❦
SCYTHE COSY

'Happy birthnight!' cried Amelia as Grimaldi Reaperton opened the door of his family barge.

'Ameeeelia!' said Grimaldi. 'Florence and Tangine are already inside . . . You'd better hurry before Tangine eats the WHOLE bowl of snail-tail snotcorn!' Then he caught sight of Vincent in his coffin pram. 'Oh, hello, Vincent!'

Amelia shuffled awkwardly. 'I had to bring him along, I hope you don't mind,' she said. 'Mum, Dad and Wooo all have the Frankenflu, so there's nobody to look after him. And I wasn't going to miss your birthnight for the world!'

'It's fine!' Grimaldi said, happily ushering Amelia into the barge, with Squashy bouncing behind her. 'The more the merrier!'

Amelia wasn't so sure Grimaldi would still feel that way after a few hours with Vincent, but she smiled and nodded anyway.

Countess Frivoleeta had called ahead to ask Grimaldi's parents if they would keep an eye on the baby. So as well as making a delightfully deadly birthnight dinner for Grimaldi, Grimardo and Grimelda had made

Vincent a special bowl of mashed brain. Much to Amelia's embarrassment, her brother farted constantly, so that the room was soon filled with a disgusting smell. Everyone pretended not to notice.

'He's getting so big,' cooed Grimelda, tickling Vincent under the chin. 'Aren't you just the cutest? You must be one very proud big sister, Amelia.'

Amelia didn't feel very proud of Vincent at that moment. Luckily her mouth was too full

to answer. She smiled and carried on munching her chocolate-covered eyeball dessert.

A few moments later, Grimardo donked his scythe on the ground twice. 'Present time!' he sang. The friends cheered.

'WOOOOO! THE BEST PART!' said Florence Spudwick. Florence was a huge, rare breed of yeti (NOT to be confused with a beast). She rummaged around under the table and pulled out a small parcel. 'WRAPPING PRESENTS ISN'T MY SPECIALITY,' she said sheepishly. 'THE ONLY RAPPING I'M GOOD AT IS IF IT'S IN A SONG.'

Vincent tried to grab the present as Florence passed it over. 'NOT FOR YOUR STICKY PAWS, YA MUNCHKIN!' Florence chuckled.

Grimaldi tore open the paper and pulled out what looked like a misshapen bobble hat. 'Oooh, thank you, Florence!'

'What is it, my little petrifying pickle?' asked Grimelda, leaning across the table.

Grimaldi studied the strange object. 'Um, Florence . . .?'

'IT'S A SCYTHE COSY!' said Florence. 'LOOK . . .' She grabbed Grimaldi's scythe and placed the hat on the blade. 'KEEPS IT NICE 'N' WARM, Y'SEE.'

'Well, I never knew I needed one of those until now,' said Grimaldi with a grin.

'My gift next!' said Tangine, standing up dramatically. He flicked his mop of glittery white hair and fluttered his eyelashes. Prince Tangine La Floofle the First was the future king of Nocturnia. As well as thinking himself one of the greatest creatures alive, he was also one of Amelia's greatest friends. 'Grimaldi, darling, you WILL love this. And this is most definitely something you NEED.'

He handed over a very neatly wrapped

package. Grimaldi opened it and studied the decorative label on the shiny-looking can. 'Pop . . . up . . . wardrobe?' he read out loud. 'I . . . I don't know what to say.'

'It does exactly what it says on the tin,' said Tangine happily. 'You press the little button on the top and POOF, there's your own portable wardrobe whenever you need it! I took the liberty of filling it up for you.'

Grimaldi put the pop-up wardrobe tin down carefully so as not to trigger it. 'Erm, thanks, Tangine!'

'My turn,' said Amelia, feeling very excited. She reached under her chair, where she'd been hiding Grimaldi's gift . . . but it was gone.

'Where is it?' she said, confused.

'Galloping gooseberries!' cried Grimelda, 'and where's Vincent?'

His chair was empty and Amelia tried hard not to scream with frustration. 'He's probably just rolled off – and I think he's taken Grimaldi's present with him. Let's check the toilet and the bin. He loves finding the yuckiest places to hide.'

'THAT'S SOME STEALTHY SPEED-ROLLING!' chuckled Florence, checking the bin.

'He does it ALL the time!' said Amelia.

'*Found him!*' came Grimardo's relieved voice. 'You were right, Amelia . . . he *was* in the toilet, the sneaky little bean!' He returned carrying Vincent, who was now covered in toilet water and happily chewing on a small black box . . .

'Sorry it's a bit sticky,' said Amelia, prying the box out of Vincent's grip and giving it to Grimaldi. 'I made it,' she said, handing over her gift. Grimaldi gently untied the string.

Everyone watched eagerly as the young reaper opened his present. He reached inside.

'Do you like it?' asked Amelia.

Grimaldi passed her the box. Inside was a pile of broken pieces of clay. Amelia stared at the ruined gift in silence.

'Is it an abstract piece?' asked Tangine curiously.

Amelia lowered the box. 'I just need to use the toilet,' she said quietly, before swiftly leaving the room.

There was a gentle knock on the door.

'Amelia?' came Grimaldi's voice. 'Are you OK?'

Amelia tried to make it look as if she hadn't been crying. She opened the bathroom door and forced a smile. 'Yep, I'm fine!' she said in an unnaturally high voice.

'Oh, Amelia,' said Grimaldi, giving her a hug. Grimaldi was exceptionally good at hugs, and sometimes all you really needed was a cuddle.

Amelia leaned her head on Grimaldi's shoulder. 'In case you were wondering, that crushed mess was actually the four of us standing under our favourite petrified tree. I spent ages making it out of eye-crust clay.' She sniffed. 'Vincent ruins EVERYTHING. I just wanted to give you the perfect present.'

Grimaldi shook his head and smiled. 'Amelia, that's the nicest thing anyone has ever done for me.' He passed her a tissue. 'We can fix it together. It'll be fun! Now come on, let's go watch the new Toadstar film!'

CHAPTER 3
EVERYTHING WAS PERFECT

The friends snuggled up on Grimaldi's bed to watch Toadstar: Toadally Awesome, whilst Grimaldi's parents took care of Vincent in the unliving room. But it was hard to enjoy the film with Vincent's loud screams echoing through the barge. Grimelda floated into the bedroom holding the distressed baby, looking rather distressed herself. Vincent held out his arms, making grabby hands at Amelia.

'I think he wants to be with his big sister,' said Grimelda. 'He rolled into the bin and got leftover dinner all over him, so I've popped his clothes in the wash and I've put one of Grimaldi's old toad onesies on for now . . . I hope that's OK.'

'Thank you, Mrs Reaperton,' said Amelia, taking the gurgling baby vampire. As soon as Vincent was in Amelia's lap, he stopped crying and started trying to eat her hair. She frowned at him and said, 'Vincent Fang, you *really* need to stay quiet whilst we watch this film, okay?'

Vincent screeched back at her with joy, a bubble of snot slowly emerging from his left nostril.

'Maybe this will keep him amused?' said Grimaldi, handing Vincent a Toadstar toy. Vincent immediately began to gnaw on the toy's head.

'Oh no, Vincent, you mustn't –' Amelia objected, but Grimaldi waved a hand.

'It's fine,' he said. 'Let him keep it if he

wants . . . I have two of those.'

'Thanks, Grimaldi,' said Amelia.

They clicked PLAY on the film, but Vincent squealed excitedly every time Toadstar appeared on the screen, and he was in *every* scene. He kept pointing at his Toadstar toy and then back at the television screen, getting louder and louder.

'Shhhh, Vincent, yes it's Toadstar . . . but you have to be quiet,' said Amelia desperately. But then Vincent threw up EVERYWHERE. So the film had to be stopped.

'WHY DON'T WE READ SOME COMICS INSTEAD?' Florence suggested.

As the friends took turns to read from a TOADSTAR comic, Vincent grabbed the pages and ripped them.

'Seriously, Vincent, you're ruining *everything*!' shouted Amelia. The baby vampire's eyes grew wide and filled with tears.

'No, no, don't start crying,' Amelia pleaded.
But it was too late. Vincent's wails rattled the
windows and made the whole barge sway.

'I FINK MY EARDRUM JUST POPPED . . .'
said Florence, covering her ears with her
huge, fluffy paws.

'All of this noise is going to make my hair
frizzy!' cried Tangine.

'Why don't we go for a walk?' suggested
Grimaldi. 'Perhaps some fresh night air
would be good for everyone.'

'It's particularly good for the nose pores,' said Tangine, who'd been applying face cream at every opportunity.

Once Vincent was tucked up in his coffin pram, snug in his fluffy toad onesie, Amelia and her friends set out into the low mists of the Petrified Forest. The Reaperton barge was docked on the River Styx in a beautifully gloomy part of the wood. The full moon shone through the trees as the friends strolled through the crispy dead leaves.

It was so peaceful. Then Amelia realised something. Vincent wasn't crying. He was finally fast asleep!

Florence glanced over with a glint in her eyes and said, 'FANG, ARE YOU FINKING WHAT I'M FINKING? ZOMBIE TAAAAAG!!'

Amelia parked up the coffin pram next to a tree. Vincent was still fast asleep, hugging his new Toadstar toy. She could finally have some baby-free fun! Moments later, the friends and Squashy were running around, playing a game of extreme zombie tag. It mostly involved finding zombies and high-fiving them without knocking their limbs off. You lost points for every fallen limb. As Amelia caught her breath, she took a moment to take in the fresh night air. For the first time that night she felt relaxed. It was just Amelia and her best friends. Everything was *perfect*!

But then Grimaldi's die-phone started

to buzz. 'Oh, *pleeease* don't let this be a squished toad alert . . . Not on my birthnight,' he said, taking the phone out of his pocket. 'Oh, someone is *calling* me,' he said looking confused. 'That hardly ever happens . . .

'Erm, hello?' said Grimaldi. 'Oh, hi, fountess, I mean Mrs Crivoleeta . . . Um, hold on . . . Amelia, it's your mum.' Grimaldi passed over the phone. 'Why can I NEVER get her name right?' he muttered.

'Hi, Mum,' said Amelia. 'How are you feeling?'

'I feel like a slug in salt water, darkling,' croaked the countess. 'Your dad and Wooo are both feeling a little better though. I hope you're having fun with your friends?'

'I am now,' said Amelia happily. Squashy squeaked once and waggled his stalk from side to side. 'Squashy says hello too!'

'What a good little pumpkin,' said Countess Frivoleeta. 'And how's Vincent?'

'Vincent's just fine,' Amelia said, strolling over to his coffin pram.

But Vincent's pram was empty.

CHAPTER 4

WE'RE TOADALLY READY

'Amelia?' came Countess Frivoleeta's voice from the handset. 'Darkling? Are you there?'

'Errrm . . .' Amelia hesitated, her eyes wide.

Florence took the phone from her. 'AMELIA JUST 'AD TO, ER, GO CHANGE 'IS NAPPY,' she fibbed and hung up.

Amelia blinked hard and took a deep breath. 'Okay . . .' she squeaked. 'He probably just rolled off . . . Let's search EVERYWHERE.'

Amelia, Florence, Grimaldi and Tangine searched the forest high and low for baby Vincent. Squashy bounced and sniffed around

every corner, through the leaves and amongst the tree roots.

But Amelia's baby brother was nowhere to be seen.

'Viiiiiinceeeent!' she called out.

'VIIIIIINCEEEEENT!' Florence yelled.

'Here!' shouted Tangine. Amelia ran over with Squashy following close behind and saw Tangine pointing at the ground. 'Look . . . the leaves are parted and flattened, like something has been rolling through them. And it's all sticky and a bit stinky!'

'Follow that trail!' said Amelia urgently, sprinting along the path. Her heart thumping in her chest, she ran and ran – but then the trail stopped. It had led them to a large cluster of strange-looking curly plants. There was a wooden sign saying, 'TOADS ONLY BEYOND THIS POINT', and underneath the sign was Vincent's Toadstar toy. Amelia gasped and

was about to step through the curly plants, but Grimaldi stopped her, looking worried.

'Um, Amelia, stop. These are toadreeds,' he said. 'Only toads can go through here.'

'*What do you mean?*' asked Amelia, feeling confused. 'But Vincent's gone that way!'

'WHY CAN'T WE GO FRU?' asked Florence, looking from Amelia to Grimaldi.

TOADS ONLY
BEYOND THIS
POINT

Grimaldi twizzled his cloak hood nervously. 'Through the toadreeds is where reapers send squished toads to start their second life . . . Like toad paradise.' He nodded towards the sign. 'It's strictly *toads only*.'

'Pottering pumpkins,' said Amelia, feeling horrified. 'I was supposed to look after Vincent, and now he might be lost in toad paradise!'

'He might *not* be! There's one way to find out for sure.' Grimaldi shuffled around in his pocket and pulled out his die-phone. He pushed some buttons and the screen filled with numbers.

'There,' he said, pointing at a column of figures. 'That number represents the total number of toads swept up in the last night and day . . . And the number next to it is the total number of toads to have been sent *through* the toadreeds in the last night and day . . .'

'Why is it flashing red?' asked Tangine.

Grimaldi gulped. 'Because the numbers don't match up. It's telling us that one extra has gone *through* the toadreeds . . .' The friends looked at each other in silence.

'Vincent,' Amelia whispered. *'We have to go after him!'*

'But Amelia,' said Grimaldi, his eye holes wide with worry. 'Once you go through the toadreeds, there's no way of getting back . . .'

'I'm not leaving my brother,' said Amelia. She stepped forward, ready to push through the reeds, but a big, hairy hand pulled her back. 'Florence, I have to go and save him!' said Amelia, her voice wobbling.

'I'M NOT STOPPING YOU,' said Florence. 'BUT YOU'RE NOT GOIN' ALONE.' Squashy squeaked and bounced up and down. 'LOOKS LIKE SQUASHMEISTER IS JOINING US TOO . . . 'OW ABOUT YOU GUYS?'

Florence looked at Grimaldi and Tangine.

Grimaldi braced his scythe. 'I'm in. But beyond the toadreeds is strictly *toads only* . . . and we don't *look* like toads . . .'

Tangine stepped forward and put his hands on his hips. 'We don't look like toads YET! I think now is the perfect time to put your new pop-up wardrobe to use.'

'DO YOU REALLY FINK THEY'LL FALL FOR THIS?' asked Florence, adjusting a green top hat with two paper eyes stuck to it. She was also wearing a green suit and a green ruffled collar.

'Of course!' said Tangine. He was wearing a green polka-dot cape, a tall crown with a green mask over his eyes and was brandishing a tall staff.

'I'M PRETTY SURE YOU DON'T NEED THAT STAFF,' said Florence.

'A future king ALWAYS needs a staff, dear Florence,' said Tangine. 'Especially when he is disguised as a toad.'

Grimaldi had a green blanket draped over him with two holes cut out to see through. He resembled a green ghost. Amelia was wearing a green stripy onesie with paper eyes stuck on to it.

'Why are there so many green things in this pop-up wardrobe?' asked Grimaldi.

'I felt you needed a fresh burst of SPRING COLOUR,' said Tangine, waving a hand. 'You always wear a black cloak. Don't you ever get BORED?'

Grimaldi shuffled awkwardly. 'I like black cloaks. They're comfy.'

'Well,' said Tangine. 'Sometimes you must sacrifice comfort to be FABULOUS.'

'How can we make Squashy look more like a toad?' asked Amelia as the orange and VERY un-toad-like vegetable bounced around her feet happily.

Tangine smiled. 'I have just the thing . . .' He whipped out a make-up bag full of various face creams. 'Hmm, where is it? Oh yes. Here!' He held up a packet labelled GREEN MOULD FACE MASK.

He squeezed out the entire contents of the bright green liquid and smeared it over Squashy's body. As the cream sank in, Squashy slowly began to turn a dark shade of green, making him look more like an unripe tomato than a pumpkin. 'There,' said Tangine. 'We're TOADALLY ready.' He chuckled at his own joke.

The friends – now disguised as *very* odd-looking toads – braced themselves at the edge of the toadreeds. 'You ready?' asked Amelia.

'TEAM TOAD IS READY TO RESCUE VINCENT!' yelled Florence.

'I was born ready!' said Tangine.

'I'll never be ready,' whispered Grimaldi. 'But I like that we're Team Toad . . .'

Squashy squeaked and then the friends bravely walked through the toadreeds.

CHAPTER 5

TOADS DON'T FART

Everything went blurry and dark. Amelia felt herself spinning round and round, then falling, falling, falling.

'EEEEEEERGH, if I'd known we'd be spinning into the toad afterlife, I wouldn't have eaten five brain-curd bagels for dinner!' Tangine moaned.

The darkness eventually began to fade into light. Then with one huge *BOING* Amelia landed on a big green lily pad, followed by Grimaldi, Tangine and Florence, who made the lily pad almost fold in on itself. Squashy was the last to appear, arriving

with a slimy green SPLAT. Tangine puffed out his cheeks.

'WELL, YOUR FACE IS THE RIGHT COLOUR FOR A TOAD NOW AT LEAST!' Florence chuckled.

The sky was a bright shade of green – and three yellow suns sat in the sky. A long line of lily pads stretched out in front of them, floating on a large body of emerald water. Each lily pad was full of toads, and they all looked like they were waiting for something. 'Squashy, I've a feeling we're not in Nocturnia any more . . .' muttered Amelia.

'Hellooo there!' said a voice, making Amelia jump. A jolly toad wearing a chef's hat and an apron was perched on the edge of the lily pad. 'You're an . . . *interesting* looking bunch,' she giggled. 'I'm Freda Frumpton.

Recently got squished by a large loaf of bread.
I was a baker *Above* the Pond you see. I made
the BEST raisin rolls.'

As Amelia looked at Freda curiously, it
suddenly dawned on her that they were all the
same size. The friends had shrunk to the size
of toads! Squashy was now even tinier.

Amelia was about to ask if Freda had seen an even smaller toad arrive recently, when a loud nasally voice echoed across the pond.

'*RIBBIT!* WELCOME TO THE POND BEYOND! THE RIBBIT-RAIL WILL LEAVE IN FIVE MINUTES. *RIBBIT!*'

'How exciting!' said Freda.

'The toad afterlife is a bit boring if you ask me,' Tangine piped up. 'I mean, look at it . . . just a big pond with a bunch of lily pads.'

Freda chortled. 'No, silly, this is just the waiting area!' she said, pointing to a large, floating sign which read 'THE POND BEYOND WAITING AREA' in glowing letters. 'The best is yet to come! I was never afraid of getting squished you know. I've heard that the Pond Beyond is WAY better than life Above the Pond.'

Amelia was too distracted to listen properly. She craned her neck, trying to see if she could spot Vincent. But there were too many toads of all different shapes and sizes. Freda carried on chatting away. 'Although, rumour has it, there's a *ferocious* toad-beast that comes out at night-time . . .'

Florence twitched. 'WHAT DID YOU SAY?' she said.

Freda smiled sweetly. 'A *ferocious* toad-beast –'

'I AM NOT A BEAST!' Florence blurted out. 'I'M A RARE BREED OF –'

'TOAD!' Amelia cut in. 'And a little confused *aren't you*, Florence? Y'know what, maybe we should change the subject,' she added quickly.

'DING DING DING! THE RIBBIT-RAIL IS OFF! MAY YOU ENJOY YOUR SECOND LIFE IN THE POND BEYOND!' said the loud nasally voice.

'Where is this ribbit-rail?' asked Amelia. 'I don't see a train anywhere –'

The lily pad Amelia and her friends were sitting on began to move. All the other lily pads, each full to the brim with toads, also started to float along the water in one long lily-pad trail.

'I do believe we're ON the ribbit-rail,' said Grimaldi, holding on to the edge of the lily pad for dear life even though it was moving very slowly indeed.

As the ribbit-rail moved along, it passed large rocks carved to look like toads. The nasally voice spoke again. 'IF YOU LOOK TO

YOUR LEFT AND RIGHT, YOU MIGHT
RECOGNISE SOME OF OUR MOST
FAMOUS RESIDENTS. SIR TOMBO TOAD,
TOADICULAR TINKLES AND DOCTOR
TOADICUS. THIS IS KNOWN AS THE
VALLEY OF THE FALLEN FROGS.'

Funny music started to play. It sounded like
a group of toads singing with incredibly deep
voices. Then Amelia realised it *was* a group of
toads singing with incredibly deep voices.

BOM BOM-BOM
BOM BOM-BOM
BOM BOM-BOM BOM BOM.

A toad chorus was standing upon the rocks, their deep croaky voices ringing out across the valley.

'I'm loving this tune!' said Tangine, singing along tunelessly.

The ribbit-rail sailed on further into the Pond Beyond. The toad chorus turned into a full-blown fanfare. Toads and frogs of all shapes and sizes played trumpets and tubas and trombones to welcome the new arrivals.

'If I were a real toad, I'd want to get squished over and over!' said Tangine, wiggling his hips along to the music.

'Shhhh!' squeaked Grimaldi. 'We can't let anyone know that we're not . . .' he whispered, *'real toads.'*

Amelia leaned out as far as she could, trying to spot Vincent on the lily pads ahead of them. But it was impossible to tell who a real toad was – and who might be a baby dressed in a toad onesie.

The ribbit-rail began to slow down, and the Land of the Pond Beyond came into full view. The water was speckled with sparkly green algae. An entire network of lily-pad towns were neatly dotted around the large pond, each connected by floating pebble pathways. Water lettuces decorated the twinkling water like pretty rotating flower boats for toads to lounge around in, and on the biggest lily pad of them all stood a large green castle surrounded by curly pond weed and tall bulrushes. Everything was spick and span. Toad butlers in bow ties were scurrying around the place, polishing the pebbles and scrubbing the building walls. Amelia saw one toad accidently drop half a lemon –and within seconds, a toad butler had hopped over and swept it up.

'Wow. Toads are a *very* tidy bunch . . .' said

Amelia. She imagined how much Vincent would LOVE to gnaw on the shiny pebbles, making them all slobbery, or smear his gooey hands over all the sparkly clean houses . . . Suddenly, Amelia felt sad and she longed for Vincent to be there with her.

'This is not what I expected,' said Tangine. 'I always thought toads were messy creatures, who loved bogs and swamps and slime.'

'Quite the opposite,' said Grimaldi. He leaned in so that Freda couldn't hear. 'They're actually some of the cleanest creatures around. I read that in a book called *Toads and Tribulations*.'

'Vincent definitely *won't* blend in as a toad . . .' said Amelia quietly.

'Well, since you're the toad expert here, Grimaldi, what else should we know?' asked Tangine. 'We need to blend in as best we can, so as not to attract attention whilst we search

for Vincent.'

Grimaldi scratched his head in deep thought. 'Hmmm. Well, they're great opera singers, but they prefer to listen to jazz. They *love* anything lemon-flavoured . . . aaaand they are usually colour-blind.' He nodded once before adding, 'Oh, and toads don't fart.'

'WHAT?' Florence blurted out. 'THAT'S THE STUPIDEST FING I EVER 'EARD. SO, WE CAN'T FART AT ALL WHILE WE'RE 'ERE?'

'It's probably for the best,' said Grimaldi. 'We don't want to give ourselves away.'

'But farting is what Vincent does best!' said Amelia, feeling very worried. 'What happens if a non-toad is found in the Pond Beyond?'

'*A non-toad, hmmm?!*' said a posh voice. A very stern toad wearing a smart uniform and a

ridiculously tall, feathered hat was standing on a dock. He was wearing a name badge that read FORTESCUE. He looked at Amelia suspiciously. 'We don't have any non-toads here . . . *do we*?'

⟨ CHAPTER 6 ⟩

ABSOTOADALLY FROGULOUS

The ribbit-rail stopped and all the toads (and pretend toads) hopped off on to the main lily pad. Fortescue stared at Amelia and her friends with furrowed eyebrows. 'Well?' he said.

Amelia gulped. Then Tangine stepped forward confidently.

'Don't be preposterous! We're totally NOT a vampire, yeti, reaper and PRINCE in disguise!' he said, putting his hands on his hips proudly. 'We are one-hundred per cent TOAD.' Amelia sighed, wishing Tangine would stop talking.

'And,' Tangine continued, pointing

at Squashy, 'this is definitely not a pumpkin. Just another normal toad with no arms and legs . . .'

Fortescue the toad guard looked Tangine up and down. 'I know you . . .' he said with a frown. 'You're that royal one . . .'

Uh-oh, thought Amelia. *BUSTED ALREADY?*

Tangine's sickly-green face turned pale.

'You're the one from that show,' said Fortescue. 'It used to be on every Sunday night Above the Pond . . .' He called over to another toad guard. 'MONTAGUE! What was the name of that show – the one with the royal toad and that silly frog wizard?'

'*Absotoadally Frogulous*?' Montague replied.

'ABSOTOADALLY FROGULOUS!' bellowed Fortescue. 'That's the one!'

Amelia, Tangine, Florence and Grimaldi looked at each other, then back at Fortescue.

Freda squeeed. 'I recognise you TOO!' she said joyfully. 'You're the one who played Princess Frogella Toadacious the Fifth!'

Other toads who were disembarking the ribbit-rail began looking over at Tangine.

'We shouldn't draw too much attention to ourselves . . .' squeaked Grimaldi from underneath his green blanket disguise.

But Tangine, who LOVED being the centre of attention, raised an eyebrow and lifted his staff. 'Why, YES,' he said confidently. 'It is I, Frogella Toadacious the Fifth.'

Amelia rolled her eyes and tugged at Tangine's cape urgently. 'This is no time for showing off, Tangine. We *really* need to go find Vincent!'

A little while later, after Tangine had signed a few autographs and answered some questions about what fame was like, Amelia and her friends were finally free from the crowds.

'TANGINE,' gasped Florence. 'WHERE DID YOUR BODY GO?!'

Tangine patted himself down, looking horrified. 'What? What do you MEAN? WHAT IS THE MEANING OF THIS?'

'OH, SORRY,' said Florence flatly. 'I JUST COULDN'T SEE IT BENEATH THAT BIG 'EAD OF YOURS.'

Tangine frowned and pointed his staff at Florence. 'How DARE you insult Princess Frogella Toadacious the Fifth,' he said.

'GUYS!' said Amelia, stepping between Florence and Tangine. 'We're not here to squabble and wave staffs around like royal toads from silly TV shows! We're here to find Vincent!' She took a deep breath and sighed. 'He could be anywhere,

and it's all my fault he isn't safe in Nocturnia.'
She looked at her feet.

'We're sorry, Amelia,' said Tangine, putting a hand on her shoulder. 'I really do let my big head take over sometimes . . .' He winked and Amelia gave a small smile.

'I'm just worried about Vincent,' she said. 'I feel like such an awful big sister.'

'COME ON,' said Florence, taking Amelia's hand. 'LET'S GO GET YOUR BRO!'

Before they could carry on with the rescue mission, the friends were stopped in their tracks by Fortescue, who handed them all a small, green envelope each. He placed the envelope into Squashy's mouth. 'Inside are your pond passes, a Pond Beyond brochure, a list of lily-pad rules and a map. Don't lose them.'

Tangine was already reading through his pack. 'RULE ONE: Don't go out at night . . .'

he read out. 'Well, that's a silly rule.'

'What happens at night?' asked Amelia curiously. Then she remembered what Freda had said about a toad-beast.

Fortescue lowered his voice. 'Ferocious Furgus skulks around the streets when the suns go down.'

'Ferocious Furgus?' asked Amelia with a gulp. 'What's so ferocious about him?'

The guard shuddered. 'He's a toad gone rogue!' he said. 'Leaves a trail of destruction in his wake. Rumour has it, he collects any toads caught wandering the streets and eats them for breakfast!' The toad guard's eyes grew wider and wider. 'So, your best bet is to stay inside during night hours, otherwise YOU *might* get gobbled up.'

Freda squealed in fright. But all Amelia could think about was poor Vincent. She couldn't let him get gobbled up;

she had to find him!

'*This way! This way!*'

Amelia was snapped out of her worried thoughts by a toad in a very elaborate gown, carrying a fan in one hand and a plate of hors d'oeuvres in the other. 'Follow me for the FIRST feast of the rest of your second life!' she sang.

Freda wriggled with joy and did a little hop skip jump.

Amelia took a deep breath. She was feeling overwhelmed with worry for Vincent. Where was he? How were they meant to find him when they were being hcrdcd from one thing to another?

'We just need to find Vincent as fast as we can and work out how to get out of this place,' Amelia whispered to Florence and Tangine. Squashy waggled his stalk in agreement.

Florence nodded. 'WAIT, WHERE'S GRIMALDI?' she said.

Grimaldi was politely listening to Freda talking about the expensive china plates she used to collect Above the Pond.

'GRIMALDI, WE GOTTA GO!' Florence called. She waved at Freda. 'NICE TER MEET YA, FREDDO. ENJOY YOUR FANCY FEAST.'

Freda suddenly looked very concerned.

'What? You're not coming to the welcome feast?' she asked.

'We're not very hungry,' said Amelia. She thought quickly. 'Er, we were eating a big dinner before we got squished, so we're still quite full.' This wasn't technically a lie.

'But you *must* come to the feast!' cried Freda. 'Only once you've eaten your first meal are you an official Pond Beyond member.' She looked at each of them in turn. 'I can't think of a reason WHY you wouldn't come, unless . . . well . . . unless you weren't a toad

at all!' She laughed loudly. 'But that would be ridiculous!'

There was a heavy silence between the friends before they all erupted with fake laughter. Squashy bounced up and down, squeaking.

'Oh, HAR HAR HAR, you got us, Freda!' Tangine said with a forced chortle. 'We're actually just a bunch of non-toads busting into the Pond Beyond . . . HAR HAR!'

Freda was in hysterics. 'Oh, you're so funny!' she said, drying her eyes. 'Let's sit next to each other at dinner!'

Amelia was torn. She HAD to find her brother, but if their cover was blown, she might never find Vincent. She sighed. 'Okay, I'm suddenly very hungry, I guess . . .'

Florence looked confused but played along. 'ER YEAH, HUNGER STRIKES!' She nudged Grimaldi, who nodded. 'Yep, starving!' he squeaked.

Tangine shrugged. 'To be quite honest, I'm always hungry,' he said.

CHAPTER 7
POSITIVELY PERFECT!

The feast took place in the shiny castle known as the Fort of Majestic. It was a grand affair with fifteen courses and palette cleansers in between. The plates were full to the brim with fancy lemon fondants, delicately decorated lemon pies and syrupy lemon sorbets. Everything was immaculately presented and very . . . *lemony*. Amelia felt like her face might turn inside out. She sat in between Florence and Squashy on one of two very long tables that lined the grand hall. The walls were covered in portraits of pretty lily-pad scenes. But the strangest part were the toad butlers who stood neatly around the hall.

'This place looks a bit like our thirteenth palace bathroom,' said Tangine.

But all Amelia could think about was Vincent. She scanned the toads sitting at each table, but there was no sign of the baby in the fluffy toad onesie. Worries raced through her mind . . . *What if he's been caught? What if Ferocious Furgus finds him?*

Amelia poked at her treacle-trousers tart, made from the finest corduroys in the Pond Beyond, and sneakily put her food on to Squashy's plate. Squashy nibbled on a piece of pie and, just as one crumb fell to the floor, one of the toad butlers sprang to life and swiftly ran over to sweep it up. Amelia noticed that every time someone dropped a speck of food it was *immediately* removed. Her mind raced with worrying thoughts . . . *What if they thought Vincent was SO grubby that they cleaned him away?!*

Grimaldi leaned over and whispered, 'You okay, Amelia?'

'Not really,' she replied. 'We're stuck in here, and Vincent is out there somewhere all alone. We need to leave!'

But before she could think about sneaking off, the grand hall erupted with cheers and claps. The doors at the back of the room burst open, revealing a toad with the biggest chin Amelia had ever seen. She was wearing a super-flouncy, ridiculously ruffled dress and a large, elaborate hat.

'That's Majestic Toad!' Freda whispered to Amelia and the gang. 'The Lord of the Pond Beyond if you will. Isn't she FROGTASTIC?!'

'*TOADS of the Pond Beyond!*' Majestic Toad trilled, her chin wobbling as she spoke. Another toad fanfare began to play as she strutted down the centre of the grand hall,

between the two long tables of excited food-munching toads. A butler toad hopped a few steps ahead of Majestic Toad, sweeping the floor wildly with a dustpan and brush to make sure it was EXTRA clean for her to step on. She paused beside a wrinkly-looking toad with half-moon glasses and pointed at his food-splattered tie.

'GUARDS, take him outside,' she barked. 'We can't have any of THIS . . .' she gestured to his messy tie, 'in our perfectly clean and tidy paradise, hmmm!'

'I'm sorry!' wept the toad with the splattered tie. 'I can change!'

'You will have a year of tidy training,' said Majestic Toad. 'Off you pop!'

Amelia felt her mouth gape open.

'THAT WAS 'ARSH,' Florence muttered. Grimaldi checked himself over for any signs of food, and Tangine raised his eyebrows.

'We could do with her in the palace!' he said, looking impressed.

The fanfare stopped abruptly when Majestic Toad stepped on the alter at the front of the hall. She turned around to face the rest of the toads, clearing her throat with a loud CROAK before speaking into a microphone.

'*Welcome to the beginning of your second life!*' she sang. 'You know, I've been welcoming toads to the Pond Beyond for over ninety-three toadillion, four-hundred frogollion and eighty-eight years now, and I must say, you are the FINEST-looking bunch I've ever had the pleasure of meeting.'

'That's probably because I'm here,' whispered Tangine, slurping on a lemon fondue.

'I BET SHE SAYS THAT TO EVERY NEW LOT OF TOADS,' grunted Florence. 'I DON'T TRUST 'ER.'

'Her perfume is making my eyes itch,' mumbled Grimaldi from under his green blanket.

'Some of you may have relatives already here in the Pond Beyond,' said Majestic Toad. 'And some of you may not. Any young toadlings who don't have family members here will be sent to our exquisite Toadling Towers, where a nice toad will adopt you soon.' She scanned the crowd of eager-looking toads.

Freda wriggled with excitement and poked Tangine in the arm. 'I can't WAIT to adopt a toadling!' she said to him happily. 'I've always longed for a little helper when I make my raisin rolls!'

'The Pond Beyond is a place of cleanliness, comfort, glamour and GOOD TIMES,' Majestic Toad continued. 'You'll find everything you need to know in your green envelopes. This is your paradise, and I will make sure your stay here is positively PERFECT!' she said, her voice dripping with sweetness.

Once the frogtastic feast had finished, Amelia and her friends left as swiftly as possible.

'Okay, now we HAVE to find Vincent,' said Amelia.

'But where do we start?' asked Grimaldi.

Amelia pulled out her map of the Pond Beyond and stared at the numerous lily-pad towns, each labelled with street names, shops and restaurants. 'Vincent could be anywhere,' she cried, feeling totally overwhelmed.

'I say we start HERE,' said Tangine, prodding the map. It was a large market on the lily pad next door. 'If there's food and toys involved, there's a *chance* he might be there, smearing snot over everything . . .'

'That sounds good to me,' said Amelia, feeling a bit more cheerful now they had a plan. 'Let's go.'

Amelia, Florence, Grimaldi and Tangine

made their way along a pebble pathway to a large lily pad, jam-packed with market stalls selling all sorts of toad treats and delights. Squashy kept close to Amelia so that he wouldn't get lost amongst the hustle and bustle of the crowd.

Amelia saw a stall selling posh patterned rugs and another called *The Enigma Toad* that sold jigsaw puzzles.

'Are you up for an impossible challenge, young toad?!'

the stall owner yelled a little too loudly in Amelia's face.

'Um, no thank you,' she replied politely. 'I have a hard enough challenge to complete at the moment . . .' she muttered to herself.

A larger market stall called *Ode for a Toad* captured Tangine's attention.

'Personalised poems for fifty per cent off!' he shrieked happily. 'That's a BARGAIN.'

'COME ON, FLOOF, WE DIDN'T COME TO THE TOAD AFTERLIFE TO GO SHOPPING,' said Florence, giving Tangine a nudge to move on. Tangine blushed. Then he pointed to the floor and yelled, 'SNOT!'

'OKAY, TANGINE 'AS FINALLY LOST 'IS MIND,' said Florence, shaking her head.

'No, look!' said Tangine, pointing at a trail of gloopy snot splodges on the ground. 'Vincent is ALWAYS covered in snot, right? So maybe this is his trail?'

'Oooh, I think you're on to something, Tangine!' cried Amelia, studying the slimy puddles.

'COME ON THEN,' said Florence, puffing out her chest. 'LET'S FOLLOW THE SNOT!'

CHAPTER 8

CLEAN AND TIDY AND PERFECT!

Squashy led the way, rolling through the crowds of busy toads and their shopping bags, following the snot trail. Amelia kept an eye out for any other signs of Vincent. Everyone else followed close behind, with Tangine trying VERY hard not to get distracted by all the pretty things for sale.

'Oh, HELLO again!' came a high-pitched voice. Amelia's heart sank. It was Freda. She stood in the snot trail, waving at the gang enthusiastically.

'THAT TOAD IS EVERYWHERE,' Florence mumbled under her breath.

'I just bought the NICEST house!' Freda oozed. 'It's the most glorious pink!'

'Pink is so last year, darling,' said Tangine casually.

'SORRY, NO TIME TO CHAT FREDA,' said Florence, about to barge her way past.

'– and there are beautiful blue tulips in the garden,' Freda carried on. 'It's just PERFECT and – *oh*! Excuse me?'

Squashy was nudging at Freda's ankle and squeaking loudly, trying to move her feet away from the trail of snot.

'What are you doing little toad?! Oh, and WHAT the TADPOLES is THAT?!' gasped Freda, pointing at the ground. 'Ewww, it's something horrid and sticky!'

Before Amelia knew it, a group of toad butlers pushed their way through the crowd and began to clean the snot trail away.

'No, no, no!' Amelia cried. That was their

only lead to finding Vincent!

Florence placed a hand on Amelia's shoulder and hugged her close. Then she leaned down and said quietly, 'AMELIA, WE 'AVE TO ACT LIKE WE DON'T CARE . . . IF THEY FIND OUT THE TRUTH ABOUT US, THEN WE'RE PUTTING VINCENT IN DANGER TOO.'

Amelia knew that Florence was right. She pressed her head into Florence's warm fur and watched as Freda pointed out every single patch of snot, then looked very proud of herself once it was all gone.

'Phew!' she said. 'That certainly had NO place hcre. The Pond Beyond is meant to be clean and tidy and PERFECT!'

Amelia took a deep breath. She had to get away from Freda before she totally lost her temper! 'I have something, um, *expensive* I need to buy,' Amelia said calmly.

'We'll see you later, Freda.'

'Cheerio! I'm going to adopt a toadling!' said Freda, hopping away cheerfully.

Amelia needed time to think. She ran as fast as she could through the market and hid herself under a large table covered in wind chimes. The tinkling noise was soothing. She hadn't meant to cry, but the tears came out before she could stop them.

Don't let Freda spot those tears, or she'll start trying to clean them up,' said a friendly voice. The tablecloth lifted and Tangine's face appeared. 'Can we come in?'

Amelia sniffed and nodded. The friends huddled up with her underneath the table. Squashy nuzzled into her tummy.

'I'm just so worried about Vincent!' said Amelia. 'He's sure to be farting *and* making a mess and someone will soon find out he's not really a toad! PLUS, if we don't find him before night-time then he could get eaten by Ferocious Furgus.'

'I have an idea!' said Tangine. 'I've just remembered something Majestic Toad mentioned at the welcome feast.'

Amelia, Florence and Grimaldi leaned in. 'WELL?' said Florence impatiently.

'She said that any toadlings with no family

here go to Toadling Towers. So, maybe Vincent MIGHT be there?' he suggested.

'Tangine, you're a genius!' said Amelia, sitting up straighter and trying not to bump her head.

'Although,' said Grimaldi, lifting the green blanket so that Amelia could see his face, 'sorry to sound negative, but didn't Majestic Toad say that the toadlings go to Toadling Towers to be *adopted*?'

Amelia felt her mouth go dry. Her cold heart thumped in her chest. 'You're right, Grimaldi.'

'THEN WE'D BEST 'URRY UP AN' FIND TOADLING TOWERS,' said Florence. 'THEN WE CAN BE THE ONES TO ADOPT VINCENT BEFORE SOMEONE ELSE DOES!'

CHAPTER 9

TOADLING TOWERS

Following the map, the friends ran as fast as they could to a town called 'LILY PAD OF THE VALLEY'. All of the buildings and houses were spotless, and not a single thing was out of place. Amelia noticed that even the residents were neat and tidy. A tall toad tipped his top hat as the friends passed; another wrinkly toad was knitting in a small glass conservatory and a group of younger toads were reading books together on a bench. There was no snot in sight.

'I FEEL LIKE I'M MAKING THIS PLACE UNTIDY JUST BY WALKING FRU IT,' said Florence.

A toad butler rushed over to Florence and began sweeping around her feet.

'I REST MY CASE,' said Florence with a frown.

'Even the way they cycle is perfect,' said Grimaldi, watching a toad ride by on a penny-farthing. 'I didn't even know toads COULD cycle.'

'If I really was a toad, this place would be perfect,' said Tangine thoughtfully.

'It's *eerily* perfect,' said Amelia.

'Well, I like it,' said Tangine, trailing behind as he flicked through the Pond Beyond brochure. 'Slithering serpents, there's a whole lily pad dedicated to an *Antiques Toad Show*!' he gasped. 'Imagine all the pretty things they must have there. High-class VINTAGE items.' He looked wistful.

'YOU'LL BE A VINTAGE ITEM IN A MINUTE

IF YOU DON'T 'URRY UP,' said Florence.

'There it is!' said Amelia, pointing at a pretty house covered in curly pond vines. A large sign with fancy writing on it read: 'TOADLING TOWERS'.

Row upon row of windows with neat wooden shutters lined the front of the house, and at the side was a little playground where three toadlings were gathered together, playing board games and drawing pictures. Amelia felt a pang of hope in her chest. Maybe one of them was Vincent.

She rushed over to the group, making them jump. One of the toadlings had fairy wings and a tutu, the other was wearing a stripy bobble hat and the smallest toadling had three eyes and was wearing a pair of big, spotty glasses. No sign of Vincent.

'RIBBIT!' cried the toadling with wings.

'Sorry to startle you,' said Amelia, stepping

back a little. 'My friends and I were wondering if you could help us. I've lost my little brother, Vincent.' She lowered her voice. 'I don't suppose you've seen him, have you? He has freckles and is usually covered in snot.'

The smallest toadling scratched her head in deep thought. 'Ribbit?' she said.

Amelia looked at the toadling blankly.

'Ribbit ribbit ribbit!' the toadling repeated with wide eyes.

'What is she saying?' asked Grimaldi.

'I don't know. It's probably baby language, like the gobbledegook Vincent talks,' Amelia sighed.

The toadling with fairy wings began to roll around, then bounced on to her feet again.

Amelia tried once more to explain, this time using actions and hand gestures. 'Little toad . . . freckles . . . snotty . . .' She pointed to her nose then pretended to smear invisible snot over her body.

The toadlings nodded then rolled around before jumping to their feet again. Squashy pa-doinged into the group of toadlings and started to squeak, but the toadlings just tickled his tummy.

'It's no good,' sighed Amelia. 'I don't think we'll get any answers here.'

'Wait a minute!' Grimaldi said. '*Look!*' The toadlings kept on rolling and standing up. Then the toadling with glasses picked up a drawing from the floor and held it out.

It was a scribbly sketch of the three toadlings. But there was also a fourth toadling in the picture. It had a pale face with freckles dotted over its nose, and yellow splodges all over its fluffy green body.

'It's Vincent!' cried Amelia. 'That's *him* in the picture! Which means he must be somewhere in Toadling Towers.' She was about to ask the toadlings where Vincent was when a serious-looking toad wearing a neat outfit and pointy glasses appeared.

'I'll take *that*!' she said, snatching the drawing from the toadling. She shook her head. 'Remember, a toadling must be clean and well behaved. You should draw something *nice*, like flowers, or Majestic Toad.' She stuffed the drawing swiftly into her pocket, then noticed Amelia and exhaled. 'Golly, I'm so sorry you had to see that,' she said, putting a hand on her chest and lowering her voice.

'They don't usually draw pictures of *snot*!'

Amelia frowned but nodded her head. 'It's totally fine. Do you work here at Toadling Towers?'

The toad nodded and offered a hand. 'Francesca Franelli,' she said with a smile. 'I look after the toadling orphans until they're adopted.'

'Oh!' said Amelia. 'I'd like to adopt!' Her tummy fluttered with hope.

'Sorry, dear, only grown-ups can adopt,' said Francesca.

Florence stepped forward. 'I WISH TO ADOPT,' she said in her deepest, most grown-up voice. 'I AM GROWN UP.

THESE ARE MY KIDS . . .' She gestured to Amelia, Grimaldi, Tangine and Squashy. 'AMELIA REALLY WANTS A NEW BRUVVA . . . SO WE CAME 'ERE.' She gulped and waited.

Francesca looked up at Florence and clapped her hands together twice. 'Well, jolly good then! Come on into the main building, and we'll find you the perfect toadling!'

Amelia gave Florence a thankful grin and followed Francesca into Toadling Towers. Everything inside was shiny and neat. Suddenly her heart ached for Vincent more than ever. She missed him AND his messiness so much!

'Now,' said Francesca, snapping Amelia out of her thoughts. 'You'll find a picture of each toadling in our catalogue here.' She pushed a huge, velvet-covered book across the desk. 'Take your time. Reed tea while you peruse?' she asked with a smile.

'Oh, no thank you,' said Amelia. She looked at the book cover and for some reason thought it would look much better with spider stew smeared across it.

Amelia scanned each page in search of Vincent. Some of the toads had names – and some didn't. They turned page after page, trawling through toadling after toadling.

'Well, if we can't find Vincent, I think we should adopt this one,' said Tangine, pointing to a teeny-weeny toadling with big happy eyes. 'I like her name... Eva Grace Cunningham Oaks. OR there's always the lovely Susan next to her. See, we've plenty of toads to choose from!'

'TANGINE YOU BIG NOGGIN, WE'RE NOT ADOPTING ANY TOADS,' said Florence, poking Tangine in the head. 'FOCUS ON FINDING VINCENT!'

Then Amelia saw it . . . a photograph of

a little round face with a freckled nose in a toad onesie. 'It's him!' she shrieked.

'Oooh, have you found a suitable toadling?' asked Francesca.

'I DO BELIEVE WE 'AVE!' said Florence, pointing to the picture of Vincent.

Amelia felt dizzy and her heart was pounding. She'd found Vincent! Everything was going to be okay . . .

* TOADLING 5.0 *

CHAPTER 10

TOADLING 5.0

Francesca took a sip of her reed tea and shuffled over to the large book of toadlings. 'Toadling 5.0, toadling 5.0,' she muttered between hums. 'Oh yes!' she said when she saw the photo. 'I'll be right back . . .'

Once Francesca was out of earshot, Amelia squeeed and the friends embraced in a big group hug. 'We found him!' said Amelia. She took a deep breath. 'I've missed him SO MUCH. Suddenly all the annoying little things he does don't matter at all.'

'WELL,' said Florence. 'I'M SURE HE'LL BE SMEARING SNOT ALL OVER YOU IN NO TIME.'

Francesca came back into the room and

Amelia did an excitable wriggle. But she froze mid-wriggle when she realised Francesca was alone.

'Sorry, dears,' she said. 'We've had a few adoptions today and I haven't had a chance to update the catalogue. It turns out this little one was adopted just before you arrived,' she said.

Amelia frowned. 'What?' she said. 'No, he can't have been.'

'Sorry, my darling, but there are plenty of other toadlings in the pond.' She flicked through the pages. 'Finnegan here is marvellous. Such a good toad. He writes dramatic poems and he's only two years old!'

Tangine stepped forward looking interested, but Florence put out a paw to stop him.

'SO, 'OO ADOPTED VIN— ERR, TOADLING 5.0?' asked Florence.

Francesca lowered her glasses and

scratched her head. 'Hmmm . . .' She was thinking hard for what felt like a lifetime. Amelia resisted the urge to shout HURRY UP!

'Oh!' Francesca said finally. 'It was a lovely toad . . . I can't for the second life of me remember her name. She was wearing a chef's hat and an apron. She was very chatty . . .'

'FREDA!' Amelia, Florence, Grimaldi and Tangine said in unison.

'That's it!' said Francesca with a chuckle. 'Do you know her?'

'WE'RE STARTING TO,' Florence grumbled.

'Where does Freda live?' asked Amelia urgently.

'I'm afraid I can't disclose that information,' said Francesca with a smile. 'If you're not going to adopt today, may I kindly ask you to come back another time? We have a rather long queue forming.'

Amelia looked round and saw a neat line

of toads eagerly waiting to adopt. 'We *do* actually know Freda,' said Amelia desperately. 'But I've forgotten her address.'

Francesca was beginning to look agitated. 'I told you, my dear, I cannot share that information with you.'

Amelia decided it was probably a good time to leave. When Francesca turned around to pour herself another cup of reed tea, Amelia quickly took the photo of Vincent from the catalogue.

Once the friends were outside, Amelia let out a huge 'AAAAAAAAARGH!'

'What are we meant to do now?!' asked Grimaldi quietly. 'This place is HUGE. It'll take forever to find Freda's house!'

'WAIT!' said Tangine. 'Pink is SO last year!'

'WHAT YOU YABBERING ON ABOUT, FLOOF?' said Florence.

'Freda was going on about her new house in

the market,' said Tangine. 'She said it was pink! With blue tulips in the garden!'

'Tangine,' said Amelia with a grin. 'You are the BEST. Let's go and find Vincent!'

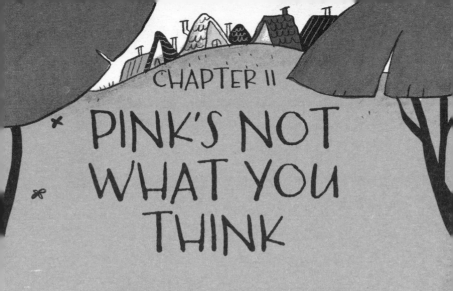

CHAPTER 11

PINK'S NOT WHAT YOU THINK

Amelia, Florence, Grimaldi and Tangine ran from one perfect lily-pad town to the next, looking for a pink house surrounded by blue tulips. Squashy rolled on ahead. Florence poked a hole in the map at each point they'd searched, so they could keep track of where they'd already been.

'How many towns have we been to?' asked Amelia.

'So far . . . eleven,' said Grimaldi.

'How many more are there to explore?' asked Tangine.

Grimaldi paused for a moment. 'Seventy-three.'

'WHAT?!' Amelia, Tangine and Florence cried. Even Squashy made a miserable squeak.

'IT'S GETTING DARK,' said Florence. 'WEREN'T WE TOLD NOT TO GO OUT AT NIGHT? BECAUSE OF THAT FEROCIOUS FURGUS TOAD ROGUE?'

'We have to carry on . . .' Amelia said desperately. 'We need to get Vincent back.'

'WE'RE IN THIS TOGEVVA, AMELIA,' said Florence. 'OF COURSE WE'LL CARRY ON LOOKING WIV YOU.'

'Wait a minute,' said Grimaldi suddenly. 'We've been searching for a pink house with blue tulips all this time. But I'd completely forgotten that *toads are colour-blind*.'

Amelia slapped a hand to her forehead.

'So, when toads see pink and blue, what are the actual colours?'

Grimaldi was silent under his green blanket for a minute. 'Sorry, I'm just trying to think. I learned a little rhyme to remember, but now I can't remember the rhyme.' He muttered words under his breath. '*A toad sees the world in a different hue . . .*' Then he gasped, 'I've got it!

'A toad sees the world in a different hue,
When something is purple, a toad sees blue.
Yellow is bright red, and orange is white,
Pink's not what you think, it's as black as the night!'

'Black!' said Amelia. 'We need to look for a black house with purple tulips.'

'Wait!' said Tangine. 'I saw that house earlier! I was thinking how the black complimented the purple flowers. Gorgeously gothic. It was back on the third lily pad we visited. What was it called?'

Amelia checked the map. 'Pad-upon-Water,' she said. 'Let's go!'

Amelia had a new surge of energy as she ran back towards Pad-upon-Water. It was getting harder to see now that night-time had fallen, but Tangine led the way.

'There it is!' he said, pointing at the house.

Amelia was about to march up to the front door, but Florence put a paw on her shoulder. 'WE CAN'T JUST GO BARGING IN, DEMANDING VINCENT BACK!'

So the friends crept round the side of the house and peered through a small window. Amelia's heart leaped as she saw Vincent, perched in a highchair at the kitchen table.

Freda waltzed in, carrying a bowl of something green and steamy with a beaker of sweet curdled milk. Amelia knew that Vincent would hate it. His favourite food was mashed

brain and he only drank lukewarm armpit sweat-shakes.

The friends watched as Vincent threw the bowl and beaker to the floor. Freda looked horrified. Vincent seized a spoon and began to chew on it, but Freda took the spoon away. Vincent began to cry. Amelia's anger at Freda was building up inside her. Freda waggled a finger at Vincent, then hopped out of the room.

'Help me climb through the window,' whispered Amelia. 'I can grab Vincent whilst Freda is out of the kitchen!'

But Vincent had his own ideas. He used his tiny bat wings to hover up and out of the chair, then darted across the table and slid down the table leg on to the floor. Then he rolled at super speed across the floor and out of sight.

'Wow!' said Grimaldi. 'That was impressive!'

Freda returned to the kitchen wearing

a pair of rubber gloves, carrying a spray bottle of ANTI-GRIME in one hand and a huge spotty cloth in the other. When she saw that Vincent's highchair was empty, she shook her head in despair and left the kitchen to search for him.

'We should knock on the door and tell Freda the truth,' said Amelia.

'WHAT DO YOU MEAN? TELL 'ER WE'RE NOT REALLY TOADS?' asked Florence.

'It's our only option,' said Amelia firmly. 'We are SO close to getting Vincent back, I don't care if she finds out about us!'

Florence grinned. 'IF THAT'S WHAT YOU WANNA DO, THEN WE'RE RIGHT 'ERE WIV YOU EVERY STEP OF THE WAY.'

Amelia marched up to the front door with Florence, Grimaldi and Tangine behind her. Squashy was having a quick poo break in the tulips.

KNOCK KNOCK KNOCK.

Freda's shadow appeared at the window and the door opened a notch. Freda's eyes grew wide. 'Frenzied froglets! *Come in!* You shouldn't be out at night!' She ushered the friends into the entrance hall. 'Don't forget to close the door behind you. I have a toadling on the loose . . .'

'SQUEAK SQUEAK!'

'Squashy?' said Amelia. She turned around to see Squashy was bouncing up and down at the front door looking very distressed . . . and the door was wide open behind him.

Without thinking, Amelia ran out of the house as fast as her legs could carry her. Vincent was rolling across the front garden, flattening the grass and flowers as he did so.

Amelia started to run, then skidded to a halt as something appeared from the shadows in front of her. Something big and slimy. The shadowy creature dragged its way along the street, with a SLOMP SLOMP SLOMP, knocking down signs and leaving a gloopy trail in its wake.

'Furgus . . .' Amelia muttered to herself. 'VINCENT!' she cried out.

But the dark silhouette of Ferocious Furgus leaned down and picked Vincent up, before turning around and hopping away into the night.

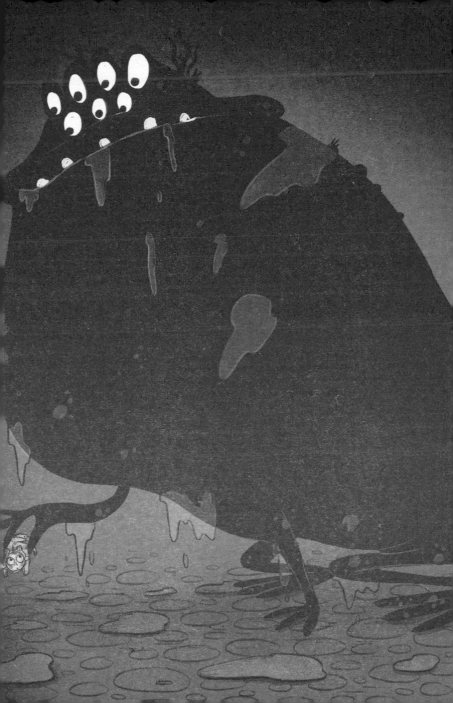

CHAPTER 12

YOU ARE NOT TOADS

'Noooooooooooooooooooooooo!' Amelia cried. Freda came running out of the house into her front garden, still wearing the bright yellow rubber gloves.

'FLEBASTIUS!' she cried out. 'MY POOR PERFECT FLEBASTIUS!'

Amelia lowered the hood of her toad onesie. Freda gasped and took a step back. 'You're . . . you're . . . not . . .' she stammered.

'No, we're not really toads and *Flebastius* is MY brother Vincent Fang. He accidentally rolled through the toadreeds into the Pond Beyond and so my friends and I came here to rescue him,' said Amelia, talking very fast. 'But now he's been kidnapped by Furgus!'

Freda looked confused. 'I . . . don't know what to say.' She shook her head in dismay. 'I was meant to adopt a lovely little toadling and we were going to have the perfect dinner together and live the perfect neat and tidy life here in the Pond Beyond.'

Florence tore off her green top hat and threw it to the ground.

'IF I 'EAR ONE MORE FING ABOUT BEING CLEAN AND TIDY AND PERFECT, I MAY HAVE TO VISIT EVERY 'OUSE IN THE POND BEYOND AND FART ON EVERYONE'S *PEEERFECT* SOFAS!' she said, clenching her fists.

Freda gasped. 'Y-you wouldn't!'

'OH, I WOULD . . . AN' WHAT'S EVEN BETTER IS, NOBODY WOULD 'EAR IT . . .' said Florence, narrowing her eyes. 'YOU'D

NEVER EVEN KNOW IT 'AD 'APPENED UNTIL THE SULTRY SCENT SLOWLY FILLED YOUR NASAL 'OLES . . .'

Freda fainted.

'OH. I DIDN'T MEAN FOR THAT TO 'APPEN,' said Florence awkwardly.

From nowhere, a toad butler rushed over and tried to sweep Freda up. In fact, lots of toad butlers were lining the street, mopping up Furgus's slime trail and straightening the signs and picket fences, ensuring the place looked as perfect as it had before.

'This is getting ridiculous!' said Tangine. 'There's wanting things to be tidy and then there's INSANITY.'

'Quick!' said Amelia. 'We have to follow Furgus's slime trail before it gets cleaned up completely. It's our only way to find Vincent!'

An alarm echoed throughout the Pond Beyond, followed by an announcement urging toads not to panic and to remain in their houses.

'DO NOT FEAR, TOADS OF THE POND BEYOND. EVERYTHING IS FINE. EVERYTHING IS PERFECT. PLEASE GO BACK TO YOUR BEDS.'

A group of toad guards marched down the street, blocking Amelia's way. A fanfare began to play as Majestic Toad waltzed along a green velvet carpet that was being unravelled in front of her as she walked.

'Well . . .' she said quietly when she saw Amelia, Florence, Grimaldi, Tangine and Squashy. 'This is a less than perfect situation. YOU are not toads.'

'I KNEW there was something bizarre about them!' shouted Fortescue the toad guard.

'What is the meaning of this?' Majestic Toad continued.

'Majestic Toad,' said Amelia, stepping forward. 'Please, you have to listen to me.

My brother accidentally rolled into the Pond Beyond, so we came here to find him. But now Furgus has taken him!'

A look of sadness flashed across Majestic Toad's face.

'You must leave immediately,' she said firmly.

Amelia raised her voice to make sure EVERYBODY could hear. 'But I can't leave without my brother! I was meant to be looking after him! He's just a baby. He didn't do this on purpose.'

Amelia felt like her heart weighed a thousand tons. Her mother's words echoed in her head . . .

'Be patient, darkling. He's not doing it on purpose . . . He adores you, you know.'

'I'm going to find my brother and there's nothing anybody can do to stop me,' Amelia said firmly. 'I'm going to find this Furgus fellow myself and get Vincent back!'

'You can't,' said Majestic Toad with alarm. 'He's a very dangerous toad.'

'Well, it's a risk I'm willing to take if it means I can save my brother,' said Amelia.

'I'M COMING TOO,' said Florence.

'I guess I am too,' said Grimaldi nervously.

'And ME, Prince Tangine La Floofle the First,' said Tangine, dramatically stepping forward. 'Yes, that's right, I'm not REALLY Princess Frogella Toadacious the Fifth.' He ripped off his mask and the toads gasped.

'You cannot do this,' said Majestic Toad with a determined look on her face. The group of toad guards stood in a long line, blocking the way of Amelia and her friends.

'I'VE DUG OVER FIVE 'UNDRED TUNNELS IN MY LIFE, AN' I CAN DO OVER ONE 'UNDRED ONE-ARMED PRESS-UPS IN UNDER ONE MINUTE,' said Florence, flexing her muscles. 'A BUNCH OF TOAD GUARDS AIN'T GONNA STOP ME.'

When the guards didn't move, Florence roared with all her might. Half of them jumped into nearby bushes and the other half fainted.

Amelia took the opportunity to RUN. Squashy speed-rolled behind her, followed by Florence, Grimaldi and Tangine. The sound of Majestic Toad's voice rang out. *'Don't doooo thiiiiiiis!'*

But Amelia ran on. She was off to rescue Vincent – and nobody was going to stop her!

'Quick!' she called to her friends. 'Follow the toad butlers with brooms . . . they're clearing away the slime trail. If we hurry, we might be able to overtake them and then we can follow the slime all the way to wherever Furgus is hiding with Vincent!'

The friends ran as fast as they could, dodging the confused-looking toad butlers and narrowly avoiding the swish of brooms and cleaning cloths.

The number of toad butlers became less and less, until the friends approached a pebble pathway and paused. There were no more toad butlers cleaning up Furgus's trail . . . but the trail was nowhere to be seen.

'LOOK!' shouted Florence, pointing to the next lily-pad town. 'THAT SHOP SIGN IS BROKEN . . . AND THE FENCE LOOKS LIKE

IT'S BEEN TRODDEN ON. FURGUS MUST'VE GONE THAT WAY.'

'And there's slime dripping from it!' said Tangine excitedly.

The friends followed the trail of destruction, passing more broken fences and snapped slime-covered signs.

'More slime!' cried Amelia as they approached a long line of gloopy splodges. Squashy bounced ahead, then squeaked. He couldn't bounce any further because the trail led straight into the water. Remnants of green slime floated on the surface.

Amelia spotted a water-lettuce boat and jumped in. Frantically, she began to paddle with her hands. Squashy bounced in too and nuzzled into her lap.

'SHUFFLE OVER!' said Florence. 'I'VE GOT OARS FOR PAWS.' She winked and jumped into the boat, almost making it topple over.

Tangine and Grimaldi squeezed in too.

'We need to follow any bits of slime we see,' said Amelia.

'ON IT!' said Florence and began to move her paws furiously.

After what seemed like a lifetime of paddling, Florence sat back and took a deep breath. 'IT'S TOO DARK TO SEE THE SLIME ANY MORE . . .' she said. 'THE WATER JUST LOOKS LIKE ONE BIG, BLACK BLANKET.'

Florence was right. The expanse of water before them suddenly felt very daunting. Amelia realised they had no idea where this Furgus even lived . . . or where THEY were right now.

The friends were well and truly lost.

·°◌ CHAPTER 13 ◌°·
TOGETHER

Amelia sat quietly whilst Squashy licked her ankles affectionately and whimpered. 'I'm sorry about all of this, Squashy,' she said sadly. Then she looked at her friends. 'I'm sorry, everyone.'

'WHAT ARE YOU 'POLOGISING FOR?' asked Florence.

'This is all my fault . . .' said Amelia. 'And Grimaldi, I've *completely* ruined your birthnight.'

'Actually, Amelia, you haven't ruined anything,' said Grimaldi, sidling up to his friend.

'Because I'm spending my birthnight with you guys.'

'But I'm the one who dragged you all into this mess . . .' said Amelia. 'If I'd been a nicer big sister and less bothered about Vincent getting in the way, we wouldn't be here. I just wanted some space away from my little brother. I realise now how selfish that sounds.'

'Amelia, you're the *least* selfish creature I know!' said Tangine.

'THIS IS ONE OF THE RARE OCCASIONS THAT I ONE'UNDRED PER CENT AGREE WITH PRINCE FLOOF 'ERE,' said Florence.

Amelia managed a small smile. She pulled out the photograph of Vincent she'd taken from Toadling Towers.

'There were times I wished Vincent wasn't always so loud and sticky and disgusting,' Amelia said to her friends, staring at the little photo. 'And I've never said this before, but I kind of missed having Mum and Dad all to myself . . .' She paused and wiped a tear from her cheek. 'But now, I wish *more than anything* that Vincent was here with me – snot, poo, farts and all.' She sighed with a heavy heart. 'I feel like a huge part of me is missing without Vincent. All he wanted was my love and attention.'

'Oh, Amelia,' said Tangine. 'I know how that feels. Sometimes I feel so empty when I'm not with Pumpy, but most of the time it's just because I'm hungry.'

Amelia looked out at the endless night before them. 'I just hope we can do this . . .'

'We'll get through it,' said Grimaldi with a smile. 'As long as we're together we can do ANYTHING!'

Grimaldi wiped a tear from Amelia's cheek and leaned on her shoulder. 'Y'know what?' he said. 'Something weird clearly happened to me when I entered the Pond Beyond . . . I'm being optimistic!'

The friends burst out laughing and hugged each other tightly.

'You're the driving force of Team Toad, Amelia,' said Grimaldi, linking arms with her.

'We WILL save Vincent and face this Furgus horror and get through this *together*. Like we always do.'

'TOGEVVA,' said Florence, fist-pumping the air.

'Togetheeeeer!' sang Tangine a little too melodramatically.

'Together,' Amelia repeated with a smile. 'LIGHT!' she blurted out suddenly.

'Yay! LIGHT!' Tangine cheered. 'Hold on . . . what?'

'Over there!' Amelia pointed into the darkness. Sure enough, a teeny speck of light glimmered in the distance. 'Florence, can you row the boat in that direction?'

'ALREADY ON IT,' Florence said, moving her paws at super speed.

As the friends got closer, Amelia saw

that it was a small lantern. Amelia squinted but before she could investigate any further, the boat hit something hard. The friends went tumbling through the air, landing with a thud on gritty ground.

'I FINK WE'VE FOUND MORE LAND . . .' said Florence, rubbing her bottom.

Amelia spat out some dirt and clambered to her feet. As her eyes adjusted to the dim light coming from the lantern, she noticed a large rock before them, with a big, gaping black hole in its centre.

'A cave . . .' said Amelia quietly.

Tangine walked slowly towards the mouth of the cave and held up a hand to tell the friends to be quiet. 'Do you hear that?' he asked softly.

Amelia listened. Then she heard it.

A deep rhythmic rumbling sound.

'It sounds like snoring,' said Grimaldi. 'Do you think it's . . .' he gulped, 'Furgus?'

Amelia took Grimaldi's hand. Then Florence held Tangine's.

'I guess we're going to find out,' said Amelia. 'Together.'

CHAPTER 14

A TOASTED CRUMPET

The friends crept into the cave, careful not to trip on any uneven patches of ground.

As her eyes began to adjust to the darkness, Amelia noticed something glint on the floor. She bent down and placed a hand over her mouth. It was a patch of snot . . . then another patch and another.

Amelia sped up, and then she began to see the outline of a shape. A very BIG shape.

She stopped.

Her eyes were still adjusting. She had to stop herself from crying out when she saw a smaller shape curled up next to the big one.

There, in his fluffy toad onesie, was Vincent.

Amelia turned to her friends. 'I have to get him . . .' she said quietly.

'What if we wake Furgus?' said Grimaldi anxiously.

Florence stepped forward. 'MAYBE IT'S TIME I PRANCED?'

Florence was an extraordinary prancer. Even though she had a rather large and bulky frame, she could prance as if she were as light as a feather.

Amelia took a deep breath. She trusted Florence with all her heart. She nodded once and watched as Florence poised herself on one toe. Then she pranced and pirouetted across the cave floor without making so much as a sound.

As the rare breed of yeti moved towards the monster with elegance and gracefulness,

Furgus stirred and Florence stopped dead. She waited as his arm hugged Vincent even closer into his chest and then turned over.

Amelia felt as if her heart had stopped beating as Florence skipped and hopped across the rocks, around Furgus's feet and around the other side out of sight. Amelia curled her hands up tightly, digging her nails into her palms. 'Please, please don't wake up,' she whispered to herself.

Seconds felt like lifetimes as Amelia waited for Florence to emerge. The toad-beast shuffled again, snored loudly, making himself cough and splutter, and turned over so that he was facing Amelia once again. Vincent was still in his arms fast asleep.

Florence was mere inches away from Furgus now. She leaned forward and stretched her arms out towards Vincent.

Then Furgus opened one huge eye.

Amelia felt all the blood drain from her face. Grimaldi grabbed Tangine's hand and Squashy rolled upside down.

'WITH BUTTTTTER!' Furgus mumbled. Then he closed his eye again and carried on snoring.

Amelia wasn't sure how much more her nerves could take.

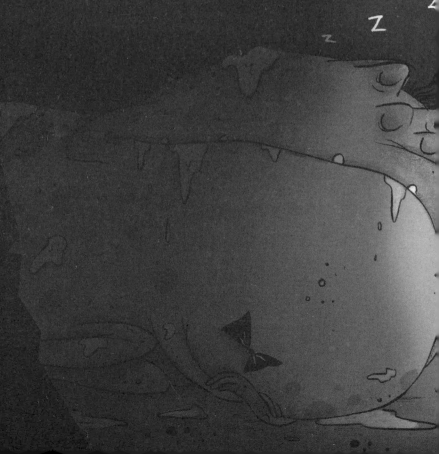

Furgus yawned and stretched his arms out wide. Seizing the opportunity, Florence leaped forward and scooped the baby up into her embrace. She pranced away just in time as Furgus brought his arms back down to his chest.

With Vincent safely curled up in her fluffy grip, Florence pirouetted once more towards Amelia and handed the sleeping baby over.

Amelia was overcome with joy. 'Vincent Fang,' she whispered. 'You little rascal.' She smiled and felt happy tears streaming down her cheeks.

She kissed his mucky face. 'I found you Vincent and I'm never ever letting go of you again.'

Vincent's eyes began to open. Amelia suddenly realised that as much as she wanted her brother to wake up and see her, right NOW was probably not the best time.

Amelia tried to tiptoe out of the cave as fast as she could. But Vincent began to gurgle, then giggle, and then laugh louder than ever before. The laughter also sounded MUCH louder inside a cave as it bounced around the rocky walls.

'Shhh, shhh, little one,' Amelia hushed. But Vincent was so happy to see his sister he kept on laughing. He hugged her neck so tightly she thought she might pass out.

'UM, GUYS,' said Florence. 'WE 'AVE A PROBLEM.'

Amelia turned around and saw that the

large shape was no longer there.

'RUUUUUUUUN!' the friends shouted in unison. Florence picked up Tangine and Grimaldi. Squashy rolled full speed and Amelia moved her legs as fast as she possibly could.

But something HUGE was blocking their way out of the cave.

Amelia stumbled backwards and Florence tripped over, sending Tangine and Grimaldi tumbling across the ground.

Amelia held on to Vincent tightly. He was still laughing, making little snot bubbles with his nose. Squashy bounced into Amelia's lap and squeaked anxiously.

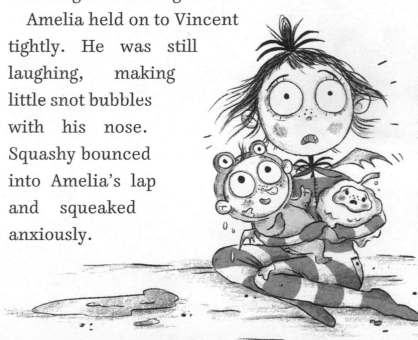

The toad-beast was dark green and covered in slime. It had multiple eyeballs that all blinked at different times, and slobber dripped from its mouth. It looked very hungry indeed.

'I'm not going to let anything happen to either of you,' Amelia said to her brother and the little pumpkin.

Florence and Grimaldi ran over and wrapped their arms round Amelia protecting baby Vincent from any harm.

'TANGINE!' hissed Florence. 'GET OVER HERE!'

But Tangine wasn't listening. He stood up, dusted himself down and walked straight towards the huge toad-beast.

'Tangine! *What are you doing?!*' shrieked Grimaldi.

Amelia watched as her best friend came face to face with the giant toad.

'My name is Prince Tangine La Floofle the First . . .' Tangine shouted up at the toad-beast. 'And I am urging you NOT to eat my friends. To be quite honest, they wouldn't taste good. Especially Florence . . .' He turned and gave her a wink. 'And she'll most likely try to do a load of press-ups in your stomach, which would give you a terrible belly ache . . .'

'What's he doing?' whispered Amelia.

'I FINK . . .'

said Florence. 'E'S TRYIN' TO DO THE RIGHT FING . . .'

Tangine took a deep breath and put down his staff (which he'd somehow managed to keep through everything). 'I, on the other hand, am FULL of essential vitamins. My skin is super succulent due to my extraordinarily complicated skincare routine; I taste like a KING for bats' sake, oh AND I'm one hundred per cent gluten free.' He gulped. 'So, what I'm saying is, please let my friends go. You can gobble me up instead.'

The toad-beast shuffled on the spot, then leaned forward.

'NOOOOOOOOOOO!' Amelia shouted as the huge creature reached out towards Tangine.

The toad-beast's face stopped merely inches from the prince. Tangine had his eyes tightly closed. 'Please don't chew for AGES,' he said through gritted teeth.

But the creature didn't move. Instead he said in a surprisingly soft voice, 'Thank you for the offer, Tangine. But I'd much prefer a toasted crumpet.'

CHAPTER 15

MY SISTER

Grimaldi collapsed in a heap and Florence farted loudly in shock. Amelia was speechless and Vincent was still laughing. Squashy had spun around so much he'd made a small crater in the ground.

Tangine opened one eye. 'I beg your pardon?' he said in a high-pitched voice.

The cave was suddenly flooded with light as the toad-beast lit a candelabra on the wall. Now they could see the whole cave. A tattered armchair sat in the corner, next to a little table piled with books. Drawings were stuck to the walls and one framed picture hung centre stage. It was a picture of the toad-beast with a much younger Majestic Toad.

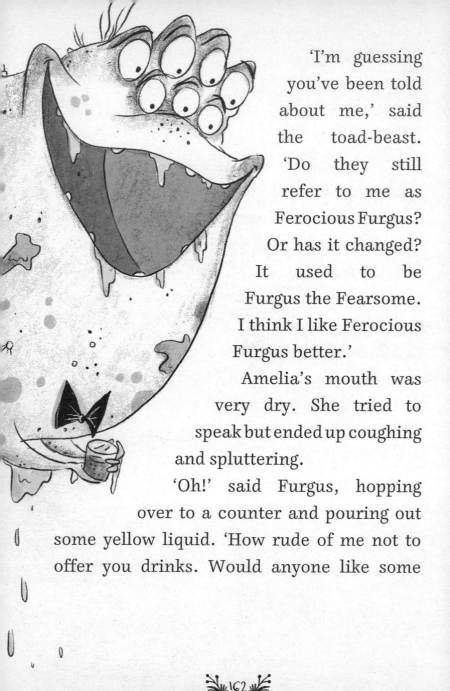

'I'm guessing you've been told about me,' said the toad-beast. 'Do they still refer to me as Ferocious Furgus? Or has it changed? It used to be Furgus the Fearsome. I think I like Ferocious Furgus better.'

Amelia's mouth was very dry. She tried to speak but ended up coughing and spluttering.

'Oh!' said Furgus, hopping over to a counter and pouring out some yellow liquid. 'How rude of me not to offer you drinks. Would anyone like some fizzy lemon juice?'

Amelia took the glass and stared at it.

Noticing her hesitation, Furgus smiled. 'It's okay. I promise I really don't plan on eating you.' He scratched his head and a large splodge of slime slid to the floor. 'I do fancy a crumpet though. Toasted, of course, with a nice dollop of butter on top. I don't suppose any of you have one?'

The friends were silent. Amelia sipped at her glass of fizzy lemon juice and felt the cold liquid soothe her dry throat. It tasted very nice and suddenly she found her voice.

'Why . . . why did you take my brother?' she asked.

'Oh, I'm so sorry. I had no idea this little one belonged to anyone . . .' said Furgus.

'You see, I only visit the Pond Beyond at night-time because that's when everyone's tucked up in bed. I usually come by to pick up some food and a few books from the Lily Library.' He gestured to the pile of books on the side table. 'When I saw the little toadling, I thought he might be lost. I guessed he'd probably run away from me, like everyone else does.' Furgus looked kindly at Vincent. 'But he giggled and smiled. So, I figured he could be my friend.' He paused and said gently, 'I haven't had a friend for a very long time.'

Vincent made grabby hands at Furgus. Amelia was hesitant at first, but the baby vampire wriggled so much that she handed him over. Furgus hugged Vincent so gently, Amelia knew for sure that he was not mean or scary.

'He's the only one who doesn't see me as a horrid toad-beast . . .' said Furgus. 'I mean,

I AM a toad-beast, but I can't help my slime problem . . .'

Tangine pointed at the framed picture Amelia had noticed earlier. 'Is that you with Majestic Toad?' he asked curiously.

'It is,' said Furgus.

'I DON'T GET IT,' said Florence. 'WHY ARE YOU LIVING ALL THE WAY OUT 'ERE IN A CAVE? WHAT DID YOU DO?'

Furgus smiled sadly. 'Oh, young beautiful yeti, the only thing I did was be myself.' He sat down on the armchair and tickled Vincent's head affectionately. 'You see, Majestic Toad is my sister.'

'Whaaaaaaaat?!' said the friends in unison. Apart from Grimaldi who was still passed out in the corner next to a dazed Squashy.

'Yes, she definitely got the looks,' said Furgus with a chuckle. 'And she had BIG dreams too. She wanted to make the

Pond Beyond PERFECT.'

'That's obvious,' said Amelia. 'But it all seems a little . . . too much?'

'My sister wanted desperately to impress,' said Furgus. 'But you see, I'm rather big and clumsy and I can't help but make slime. Whenever I was around my sister's perfect creations, I would get worried about messing something up, which would make me nervous, and then I'd get slimier . . . and then I'd end up ruining *everything*.' He straightened the picture frame, smearing slime all over it.

Amelia's heart swelled for Furgus.

'I loved her so much and I wanted everything to be perfect for her,' said Furgus. 'So, I decided to leave the Pond Beyond forever. That way, I couldn't wreck her perfect things.'

'That's so sad,' said Amelia. 'Do you miss her?'

'Terribly,' said Furgus. 'But I'm happy knowing how successful she is. She has followed her dreams to make the neatest and most perfect Pond Beyond there is!' He stroked Vincent's forehead, sending him into a sleepy daze. Amelia was amazed at how calm Vincent was around the toad-beast.

'WHY DO THE TOADS IN THE POND BEYOND CALL YOU FEROCIOUS FURGUS, THOUGH?' asked Florence. 'COZ YOU DON'T SEEM VERY FEROCIOUS TO ME.'

'Oh, you know how things get blown out of proportion,' said Furgus with a light chuckle. 'They see a dark shadow moving through the streets at night, and one rumour leads to another, until it becomes something completely different. But it's okay.'

'It's not okay,' said Amelia with a frown. 'Why don't you talk to them, like you did us? And tell them you're not ferocious? Then they wouldn't be scared of you.'

'If the toads believe I've gone rogue, then my sister won't have to worry about me,' said Furgus. 'She'll be glad I'm not around.'

'Furgus,' Amelia said. 'You have to go back.'

'Back?' he said quietly.

'Back to the Pond Beyond. Back to your sister – and your home!' said Amelia.

Furgus looked unsure. 'But I'll get slime and grime everywhere. The Pond Beyond is too perfect for a toad like me.'

'Well,' said Amelia with a smile. 'Maybe it's time for a change.'

'But change is scary!' Furgus said with a frown.

'It's often a bit scary at first,' said Amelia. 'I had trouble adapting to life with Vincent around, but when he disappeared I realised how much BETTER life was *with* him.' She sighed. 'Though I was so concerned

with *finding* him that I didn't really think about what came next – and now we're stuck in the Pond Beyond with no way of getting home!'

'Well,' said Furgus. 'Perhaps my sister can help you.' He stood up and held out a hand to Amelia. 'Come on little vampire, it's time to go home!'

CHAPTER 16

TRUMPET SOLO

The three suns had begun to rise in the Pond Beyond. Amelia helped Furgus get ready whilst Florence attempted to wake up Grimaldi and stop Squashy spinning.

'Eeeeergh,' Grimaldi groaned. Then his eyes widened. 'TANGINE!' he shrieked. 'He's about to be eaten!'

Florence chuckled. 'YOU'RE A BIT LATE TO THE GAME,' she said. 'YOU MISSED THE HEARTFELT BIT AN' EVERYFING.'

Tangine filled Grimaldi in on all that had happened (this involved a lot of dancing and operatic singing) whilst Amelia combed Furgus's little tuft of hair. 'Are you sure you're ready to do this?'

'I think so,' said Furgus. 'I really hope we can help *you* get back home too . . .'

'So do I,' said Amelia, feeling her heart ache for her mum and dad and Wooo.

Furgus twiddled his fingers nervously. 'Amelia. What if I get slime everywhere? What if I ruin my sister's beautiful things and she gets upset?'

'I'm sure you accidentally putting slime on her stuff will be the least of her worries when she sees you again,' Amelia said with a smile. She looked at Vincent, who was nibbling on one of Furgus's books and smearing snot over the pages. 'Sometimes, you don't realise how much you miss something until it's gone.'

As the friends left the cave, the waters of the Pond Beyond were positively glowing.

All the toads would soon be waking up, ready to start their new day in the lily-pad towns. But just as Amelia was about to board the water-lettuce boat, she noticed a strange rope dangling from the sky. There was an envelope attached to the end of it.

'Um, Furgus, what's that?' she asked. Then she saw the words: *For Miss Freda Frumpton* written on the back.

'Oh, it appeared outside my cave yesterday. I've no idea where it comes from or who Freda is,' said Furgus.

'How strange,' said Amelia, watching the envelope slowly spin on the spot. Then she widened her eyes. 'Wait a minute . . . Freda Frumpton. We KNOW her!'

Florence traipsed up to the envelope and grunted. 'EVEN WHEN WE'RE MILES AWAY, FREDA FINDS A WAY INTO OUR LIVES,' she chuckled.

Amelia scratched her head, thinking hard. She looked up at the rope, which seemed to disappear into the sky above. 'I've had a thought!' she said suddenly, pointing at the envelope. 'What if this envelope has come from Above the Pond?'

Furgus nodded. 'That seems plausible . . .' he said. 'Maybe someone is trying to contact Freda?'

'Exactly!' said Amelia. 'And if someone is trying to communicate from above then maybe, just maybe, they might be able to help us get back home!'

'OOOH, GOOD THINKING, AMELIA!' said Florence.

'We should take the letter with us,' said Amelia. 'Then we can give it to Freda. And when she opens it, we can find out who's trying to contact her . . . and see if they can help US.'

'YEEEEEAH!' cheered Florence, fist-pumping the air.

'Come on then,' said Amelia. 'Time to reunite Furgus with his family, then get back to *ours*.'

The friends piled into the water-lettuce boat. Furgus swam through the pond water carefully (so as not to get his bow tie wet), and pulled the little boat along. They soon reached the lily-pad towns of the Pond Beyond, and made their way towards the Fort of Majestic.

Furgus peered anxiously up at the glittering castle. 'There's no place for me here!'

Amelia shook her head. 'That's not true. Family is more valuable than anything. Come on, let's do this!' Holding Vincent tightly, Amelia joined Furgus at the castle entrance. She rang the large doorbell and waited patiently.

A toad guard opened the door and gasped. 'Wh-wh-what is the meaning of this?' he said.

'Please don't activate any alarms, there's no need to worry . . .' said Amelia.

Shrill bells sounded throughout the castle. Amelia put her head in her hands. 'What did I *just* say?' she sighed.

Furgus began to panic and slime started to drip from his elbows. 'I . . . I'm sorry, I shouldn't have come here!' he said, backing away.

'WHAT IS GOING ON?' came the stern voice of Majestic Toad. 'My morning alarm doesn't go off for another half hour . . .' She emerged at the doorway wearing her nightgown and slippers.

'Um, hello sister,' Furgus said quietly. He gave her a small wave and accidentally flicked slime on to the toad guard, who immediately fainted.

There was silence. Amelia really hoped Majestic Toad would do the right thing and welcome her brother back home.

'Furgus?' she finally said. 'I . . . I thought you'd moved away. I thought you'd turned rogue . . .'

'He wanted you to believe that . . .' said Amelia. 'Furgus chose to leave so that you could pursue your dream of making a perfect toad paradise.'

'Is this true, Furgus?' asked Majestic Toad.

Furgus nodded his head sadly. 'I just wanted the best for you,' he said. 'I know I'm clumsy and sticky, and I make the place less perfect.

But my new friend Amelia and her brother Vincent made me realise how much I miss you. And I completely understand if you don't want me here, but I thought perhaps it was worth us trying to be a family again.'

Majestic Toad was quiet for a moment. Then, to Amelia's relief, she smiled.

'Thank the bats,' Tangine whispered to Florence. 'I was worried for a second this *wasn't* going to be a happy ending.'

Amelia stepped forward to talk to Majestic Toad. 'I got so grumpy about Vincent destroying my stuff and being generally annoying. But then when he was gone, the thought of never seeing a snot-covered toy or a bum-print-covered book made my heart ache. A huge part of me was missing without my brother.'

Majestic Toad looked up at Furgus. 'I did get frustrated when you slimed up all my beautiful things,' she said. 'But I never stopped loving you. When you left, I was heartbroken. Then when I thought you'd turned into a big, scary toad-beast, I blamed myself. I thought I'd driven you to that. Then I became a little . . . *obsessed* with perfection. But I never felt truly happy. Something was always missing, and that was you.'

Furgus smiled.

'Oh Furgus, I missed you every single day and night,' continued Majestic Toad. She looked at Amelia and her friends. 'I can't thank you enough for bringing my brother back to me.'

'The extreme anxiety was worth it,' said Grimaldi.

Majestic Toad chuckled, then ran up to Furgus and threw her arms around him in a huge hug. 'You know what, I think this place could do with a bit of a change. I've been trying to make things perfect for so long now

and actually it's really hard work . . . and a bit boring!'

Amelia's heart filled with joy as she watched brother and sister unite in a big, slimy hug.

'I LOVE THIS!' said Tangine, happily dancing on the spot. He accidently kicked a splodge of slime, which went flying through the air and hit Florence between the eyes.

'OH NO YOU DON'T . . .' she bellowed, scooping up a handful of slime and throwing it at Tangine's bottom. He gasped.

There were a few moments of silence and then Florence yelled, 'SLIME BATTLE!'

Majestic Toad was one of the first to join in. She threw globules of slime at the toad guards, who soon warmed to the idea and joined in. Grimaldi and Squashy were narrowly missing slime balls flying through the air, and Amelia was having lots of fun rolling around and making slime-angels with Vincent.

Toads from the rest of the Pond Beyond began to gather, some bewildered, some confused, and some embracing this new and exciting way of life. Soon, the whole of the Pond Beyond was having a full-on slime battle.

Freda ran through the crowd in a frenzy. 'WHAT IS HAPPENING?' she cried. Then BOSH! a big blob of slime splattered

Freda right on her chef's hat. She froze on the spot and her eyes were wide.

'COME ON, FREDA, 'AVE A BIT OF FUN!' said Florence.

Freda scooped up some slime and rolled it into a ball, her expression slowly turning from shock to determination. Then she launched with all her might, throwing the slime ball high into the sky. Freda looked at Florence then burst out laughing. 'That was AMAZING!' she said. 'MOOOOORE!'

The slime battle went on for most of the morning. The friends were having so much fun that they'd completely forgotten they were still in the toad afterlife . . .

'Grieving gobblepots, we need to get back home,' said Amelia. 'Our parents will be going mad with worry!'

'But how do we get back?' asked Grimaldi.

'I'm afraid there is no way,' said Majestic Toad awkwardly. 'I'm so sorry . . .'

Amelia hugged Vincent, who was chewing on a piece of paper. 'The letter!' she said suddenly. 'An envelope addressed to *Miss Freda Frumpton* appeared on a rope outside Furgus's cave yesterday. If it's coming from the sky, then surely there's a chance it's coming from Above the Pond?'

Freda stepped forward, dripping with slime. 'Did someone say *Miss Freda Frumpton?* That's me!'

Amelia passed Freda the envelope with a smile. 'We didn't open it, but if we can find out who it's from, then we might be able to communicate with them and maybe they can help us get back to Nocturnia.'

Freda opened the envelope carefully and unfolded the piece of paper inside. It read:

Dear Freda,

We heard you got squished and we were very sad. We were regular customers at your bakery in Nocturnia and we ADORED your raisin rolls. We bought one every single night. Would you be able to pass on your recipe, so that we can continue to make your award-winning bakes up here, Above the Pond?

We weren't sure how to contact you in the Pond Beyond, so we really hope this works! If you DO get this letter, we'd love to hear from you.

Your favourite customers,

Ricky and Graham

'Ricky and Graham?!' said Amelia.

'Lovely pair of unicorns!' said Freda. 'You know them too?'

'Yes!' said Amelia, feeling a flurry of hope.

Ricky and Graham were unicorns with a knack for trying new things. They had become very good friends with Amelia since her big adventure in Glitteropolis.

'This means they must be at the other end of the rope, back in Nocturnia!' said Amelia hopefully.

'If we climb up the rope, maybe we'll end up back home?' suggested Grimaldi.

'I'm not climbing in these shoes!' said Tangine, pointing at his feet.

'I had no idea you were wearing such posh shoes this whole time,' said Amelia, a little surprised.

'Don't you know me by now? I'm Tangine La Floofle the First . . . I must *always* wear

extra posh shoes for our adventures.'

'I CAN CARRY YOU ALL,' said Florence. 'AND IF WE TUG ON THE ROPE, RICKY AND GRAHAM MIGHT PULL US UP . . .'

'It's worth a try!' said Amelia, holding Vincent in one arm and scooping up Squashy in the other.

'Remind me where this mysterious rope is again,' said Majestic Toad, looking confused.

'It's dangling outside my cave,' said Furgus. 'So, if you come with us, perhaps I can show you around at the same time,' he added with a smile.

'Sounds . . . perfect!' said Majestic Toad.

Back at Furgus's cave, the rope was still dangling mysteriously from the sky.

'DO YOU RECKON THIS COULD HOLD A

YETI, A VAMPIRE, A REAPER, A PRINCE, A BABY AND A PUMPKIN?' said Florence, studying the rope.

'I hate to be the bearer of bad news,' said Majestic Toad. 'But since it's a written rule that toads who enter the Pond Beyond cannot return Above the Pond, I'm not entirely sure what happens to those who try . . .'

'Ah,' said Amelia, raising an eyebrow. 'But remember, we're *not* toads.'

'Of course!' said Majestic Toad, waving a hand. 'Then you're probably not going to implode as you leave. Phew!' She laughed. Grimaldi's eye sockets widened.

'Okay . . . we'd better get going!' said Amelia. 'It was really lovely to meet you all.'

Furgus leaned down and patted Vincent on the head, before saying to Amelia, 'Vincent is so lucky to have such a kind-hearted sister. Thank you from the bottom of my slimy heart for making my afterlife complete. May I?' he asked, opening his arms wide.

Nodding, Amelia threw herself into Furgus's wonderfully slimy embrace.

Majestic Toad joined in and hugged Amelia and Vincent tightly. 'Thank you for bringing Furgus and me together again,' she said happily. 'Now my toad paradise truly IS perfect.'

Amelia smiled. Vincent tried to chew on Majestic Toad's cheek. 'If Vincent ever accidently rolls into toad paradise again, I'll be sure to come and visit,' Amelia said with a giggle.

As the strongest of the group by far, Florence held on to the rope tightly with one arm, then managed to hug Grimaldi, Tangine and Amelia under the other. In Amelia's arms was a very excitable Vincent and a very squeaky Squashy.

'Oh, and please do pass this on to Ricky and

Graham!' said Freda, handing an envelope to Tangine. 'It's my raisin roll recipe.'

Tangine saluted, and Florence held on to the rope with all her strength. Then she tugged it three times.

'I really hope this works,' said Amelia.

A few minutes passed and the friends and the toads waited in anticipation. Then Florence's feet started to rise from the ground. The rope was being pulled upwards and the friends were on their way home.

CHAPTER 17

RICKY AND GRAHAM SAVE THE DAY . . . AGAIN!

As the friends were lifted higher and higher into the sky, everything turned pitch-black. Amelia held on to her brother and Squashy as tight as she could. It was a very strange sensation, and yet Amelia knew she was in safe paws with her yeti friend. Suddenly, she felt something brush past her face . . .

'Reeds!' she gasped. 'Toadreeds! We must have made it out!'

Amelia took a deep breath as the rope was dragged through the tall reeds. The cold night air hit her face and the musty scent of damp forest filled her nose. The rope jolted and Amelia felt herself tumbling through the reeds, before finally skidding to a halt. When she opened her eyes, Amelia recognised the grey petrified trees, the low-hanging mist and the full moon shining down upon her.

'We're home, Vincent!' she whispered.

Vincent was so excited, he weed in her lap.

'It's fine,' chuckled Amelia. 'Totally gross, but fine.' She gave her brother a big, squidgy kiss on his sticky cheek. He yawned and Amelia watched as he slowly closed his eyes. His little freckled nose dripped with thick snot and his podgy baby belly moved gently up and down with the rhythm of his breaths.

Love overwhelmed Amelia and she found she didn't ever want to leave his side again.

Florence, Grimaldi and Tangine traipsed over, looking a little flustered, but happy.

'Is my hair okay?' asked Tangine, patting his mop of glittery locks. 'I think the Pond Beyond's humidity has made it go a bit fluffy . . .'

Florence put an arm round her friend. 'IT LOOKS LOVELY.'

Tangine frowned in response. 'I'm waiting for the part where you make fun of me . . .' he said.

But Florence just smiled and took his hand. 'YOU WERE VERY BRAVE

'Oh . . .' said Tangine. 'Well, I just wanted you to be okay. I mean, ALL of you to be okay.' He cleared his throat. 'And I'm really glad you are.'

'Well, would you look at that, Graham!' said a familiar voice. It was Ricky the unicorn. He was wearing a bucket cap with toggles and a rain jacket and holding a large fishing rod

with a rope attached to it. Sitting next to him was Graham, who was in a similar outfit and munching on a sandwich.

'You won't believe this, Graham,' said Ricky. 'But I just fished Amelia and her friends out of the toadreeds . . . Y'know, where that toad paradise is meant to be. Where we sent the envelope for Freda!'

Graham adjusted his glasses and finished his mouthful. 'Blimey, Ricky, you're right!'

TOADS ONLY
BEYOND THIS
POINT

Amelia chuckled. 'It's good to see you both . . . in fact you saved us from being stuck in the toad afterlife *forever*!'

Ricky and Graham looked at each other, then shrugged and grinned. 'Ricky and Graham save the day . . . again!'

Tangine handed the unicorns the envelope from Freda. 'Freda got your letter,' he said with a smile. 'She asked me to give this to you.'

'Oh my days, Ricky,' said Graham, opening up the letter. 'It's the raisin roll recipe! AND she's included her secret ingredient!'

Ricky made a strange honking sound. 'This is PERFECT, Graham.' He turned to Amelia and her friends. 'We opened up a new bakery in honour of Freda after she got squished. We were desperate to get her raisin roll recipe and carry on making them.'

'Yeah, we knew she would've been swept up

and sent through the toadreeds, and since we couldn't go through to speak to Freda ourselves, we figured sending a letter might work,' said Graham. 'We had no idea it would help you guys out too. What a weird and wonderful chain of events.'

'Well, in a VERY weird way, I guess we have Freda to thank for getting us back home . . .' said Grimaldi.

Amelia chuckled. 'I guess we do.'

'Wanna come to the official opening ceremony of our new bakery in a few nights?' asked Graham. 'It's going to be called *Raisin the Bakes*.'

'We'd love to!' said Amelia.

'GRIMAAAAALDI!' called a voice. It was Grimaldi's mum. 'There you are, darkling,' she said, floating through the trees. 'Time for birthnight cake!'

'WAIT,' said Florence. ''OW LONG 'AVE

WE BEEN OUT . . . PLAYING?'

'Oh, not long . . . about half an hour or so,' said Grimelda. 'Have you had fun?'

Amelia looked at Florence, Grimaldi and Tangine. Even though a whole day and night had passed at the Pond Beyond, it seemed hardly any time at all had passed in Nocturnia!

'It's been quite the game!' Amelia answered with a big grin. She looked at her friends and winked.

'That's what I like to hear!' cheered Grimelda. 'Now who'd like some birthnight cake and sweat-shakes?'

'MEEEEEEEE!' the friends bellowed.

'Oooh, YES please!' said Ricky and Graham.

Within five minutes of sitting down in the comfort of the Reaperton barge, with their bellies full of yummy cake and warm sweat-shakes, Florence, Grimaldi and Tangine had all fallen asleep in one big, cosy slump on the sofa. Vincent was asleep in Amelia's arms, lightly snoring, and Squashy lapped up any cake crumbs before falling asleep too. Ricky and Graham were discussing their new bakery business with Grimelda and Grimardo in the kitchen.

Amelia was the only one awake. She was enjoying listening to the light snores of her friends and the comforting sound of background chatter. But she soon found her eyes were beginning to droop too. She smiled sleepily as she cuddled Vincent. Everything was just as it should be. Everything was PERFECT.

CHAPTER 18

TO THE PONDS AND BEYOND

A few nights later, the *Raisin the Bakes* opening party was in full swing. Creatures from all over the kingdoms came to celebrate. Ricky and Graham had successfully baked a batch of Freda's famous raisin rolls, and Vincent tried his first scream bun. Even though most of it ended up in Amelia's hair.

Countess Frivoleeta and Count Drake were feeling MUCH better now, and Wooo was back to his wonderfully ghost-like self, keeping the Fang mansion in order and offering wise words of advice whenever Amelia needed them.

'DO YOU FINK YOU'LL EVER TELL YOUR MUM AND DAD ABOUT OUR POND BEYOND ANTICS?' Florence asked Amelia.

'I think . . .' said Amelia with a smile, 'that it's going to be mine and Vincent's little secret.'

'I like the fact that it's our secret adventure . . .' said Grimaldi. 'Team Toad's top-secret mission!'

'I do love a good secret,' said Tangine. 'I have A LOAD of them.'

'WELL, FLOOF, I'M GONNA MAKE IT MY MISSION TO FIND 'EM ALL OUT.' Florence gave him a friendly nudge.

'Darkling,' came the countess's voice. 'Your father and I are going to head back home now. Did you want me to take Vincent back with us to give you some time alone with your friends?

Amelia looked at her grubby little brother

and shook her head.

'No, it's okay. He can stay,' she said, giving her brother an affectionate tap on the nose. 'Vincent is one of the gang after all.'

'You're the perfect big sister,' said Count Drake, kissing his daughter on the head. 'Your mum and I are incredibly proud of you.' Amelia's heart felt all warm and fuzzy.

Ricky and Graham brought out a new batch of freshly baked goods, which smelled and looked DELICIOUS. 'Come fill your tummies, you horrible lot!' Ricky called out. Creatures of all types and shapes and sizes gathered and chattered and gobbled.

Then Amelia suddenly remembered something. 'Graham, I don't suppose you have any crumpets among your baked goods, do you?'

'Of course we do!' said Graham. 'How many would you like? A plateful? Well cooked or grossly pale?'

'Definitely toasted until almost burnt,' said Amelia. 'And could you spread a dollop of butter on them too please?'

'They wouldn't be complete without it,' said Graham with a wink.

When he handed the plate of freshly toasted crumpets to Amelia, the rest of the gang

appeared almost immediately. Squashy was bouncing up and down, licking his lips.

'I DO LOVE A CRUMP!' said Florence, rubbing her paws together.

'Well, they're not actually for us,' said Amelia. 'I have one more thing I need to do . . . But I'm going to need some of Ricky and Graham's rope.'

The friends stood before the tall toadreeds. The crumpets were safely stashed in a small box attached to the end of a rope with an envelope addressed to Furgus.

'Furgus finally gets his crumpet,' said Grimaldi with a giggle.

'That's not all,' said Amelia, pulling another very small box out of her pocket. 'This is for *you.*'

'Me?' said Grimaldi, looking confused. He opened the box carefully and gasped. 'It's . . . perfect,' he said with the biggest smile on his face. Inside was a little eyecrust-clay model of the friends and Squashy under their favourite tree. And this time, Amelia had made a tiny Vincent too.

Vincent screamed with delight. 'Look, it's you!' Amelia chuckled. Vincent stared at the model, then shouted, 'RIBBIT!'

Amelia gasped and her friends put their hands over their mouths.

'Well, I never,' said Amelia. 'I think Vincent just said his first word!'

'That's REALLY going to confuse your mum and dad,' Grimaldi chuckled.

Tangine raised an eyebrow and leaned towards Vincent. 'I thought we'd agreed your first word would be Tangine?' He blew a raspberry, making Vincent burst into laughter and then do a huge fart.

'FOR A TINY VAMPIRE, YOUR BROTHER CAN SURE MAKE SOME BIG SMELLS,' said Florence.

'You're right, Florence.' Amelia chuckled and hugged her stinky sibling. 'And I wouldn't have him any other way. Stench, snot and all. I love you, Vincent Fang, forever and ever, to the ponds and beyond.'

THE END

BEST FRIENDS FOREVER

pumpkin hugs from Amelia

Amelia's
favourite
memories

I ♥ PUMPKINS

Squashy and I love hugs and dancing together. This was when I realised Mum's annual Barbaric Ball wasn't as bad as I first thought!

PuMPKiNS RULE!

He and Grimaldi pranced like Creatures of the Light in the Meadow of Loveliness! We thought we'd be scared entering the Kingdom of the Light, but we soon found out it was just like our Kingdom, just a bit more sparkly!

I got to meet Florence's Grand-ye Clemence. She's SO NICE and LOVES to party even though she's 350 years old!

Tangine's outfits get more and more ridiculous over time. He's such a funny vampire-fairy!

He and my friends sat and watched the moon set whilst eating sugarplum ice creams, AND we were surrounded by some new friends called YUMPKINS!

CUTE!

Look at us go!!!

We NEVER knew Wooo rode a motorbike! Just when I thought he couldn't get any better! I love Wooo – he always gives me the best advice.

...family so much, and even BETTER because I ...e best baby brother in the ...se . . . even if he DOES cover ...thing in mashed brain and ...-prints!

♡ ANGS ♡
...REVER
xxx

AMELIA FANG

Sink your fangs into these howlingly hilarious adventures!

AMELIA FANG and the BARBARIC BALL

LAURA ELLEN ANDERSON

AMELIA FANG and the UNICORN LORDS

LAURA ELLEN ANDERSON

AMELIA FANG and the MEMORY THIEF

LAURA ELLEN ANDERSON

Complete your collection today!

DISCOVER A
WORLD OF MAGIC
BEHIND EVERY RAINBOW!

HE THRILLING NEW SERIES
BY LAURA ELLEN ANDERSON

For Ali. You wonderful
creature of the dark and light!
FANG-K YOU for believing in Amelia's
pumpkin-shaped dreams from the very first dark
and gloomy Wednesday night in Nocturnia xxx

EGMONT

We bring stories to life

First published in Great Britain in 2020 by Egmont Books

An imprint of HarperCollins*Publishers*
1 London Bridge Street, London SE1 9GF

egmontbooks.co.uk

HarperCollins*Publishers*
1st Floor, Watermarque Building,
Ringsend Road, Dublin 4, Ireland

Text and illustrations copyright © Laura Ellen Anderson 2020

The moral rights of the author and illustrator have been asserted

ISBN 978 1 4052 9769 1
Printed and bound in Great Britain by CPI Group
5

A CIP catalogue record for this title is available from the British Library

MIX
Paper from
responsible sources
FSC™ C007454

FSC
www.fsc.org